and she is now a partner in the ... old son to work with her every day.

Discover more at millsandboon.co.uk

A HOME
FOR HER BABY

ELEANOR JONES

MILLS & BOON

First Published in Great Britain 2018
by Mills & Boon, an imprint of HarperCollins*Publishers*
1 London Bridge Street, London, SE1 9GF

A Home for Her Baby © 2018 Eleanor Grace Jones

ISBN: 978-0-263-26531-6

0918

MIX
Paper from
responsible sources
FSC™ C007454

This book is produced from independently certified FSC™ paper to ensure responsible forest management.

For more information visit: www.harpercollins.co.uk/green

Printed and bound in Spain
by CPI, Barcelona

To my brother Thomas
who always reads my books

CHAPTER ONE

"I TOLD YOU it was going to get rough." Tom Roberts checked the weather warning yet again before looking back at his younger brother, his expression darkening. "I warned you, Bobby, you should never have asked her along in the first place. Night fishing in October is not a holiday jaunt. I make the decisions, remember, it's my call, and if this storm really kicks in then the last thing we need is a woman on board, especially a total rookie… Anyway, your problem, because no matter what happens there's no way we're giving up on this fishing trip."

Bobby glanced out at the raging black sea beyond the cabin window. *The Sea Hawk* was already being buffeted by the waves that crashed onto the deck. "I'll watch out for her," he said determinedly, balancing with long practiced ease as the boat lurched up beneath their feet, then plunged back down with the rolling waves.

Tom resolutely held it on course. "It's like a roller coaster," he yelled over the thumping engine and the roar of the ocean. "No…!" His dark eyes shone. "It's better than a roller coaster because it's real life."

"I'll go see where Ali is," Bobby said. "And don't worry, I'll make sure she stays off the deck."

Tom leaned across so he could hear. "Tell her to stay away from you, more like… You're only twenty, Bob. She's way too old for you and you'll only end up getting hurt."

Bobby frowned. "Don't be daft, she's just a friend… and she's married anyway. She promised to scatter her dad's ashes on the ocean…he was a fisherman, too. She'd just met him for the first time only a few months before he died and it all came as a bit of a shock. Have a heart, Tom. She just wants to do right by her dad."

"I think it's *your* heart that's the problem," Tom responded with a wry smile, focusing all his attention on the controls of *The Sea Hawk*. "She's got way too deeply into it if you ask me."

"I'm not asking you," Bobby snapped. "I'll go and see where she is."

DESPITE HAVING BEEN ordered to stay inside, Ali stood on the deck clutching her precious urn. She wanted to scatter her dad's ashes at just the right moment, a moment he'd have gloried in, when the sea was at its wildest. And surely this must be it. Holding tightly on to all she had left of the father she'd barely known, she remembered the days just before he died, when she'd sat with him and he'd opened up to her about his life. He'd told her things then that her mother never had; the things she'd always wondered about.

Allowing herself to sway with the movement of the boat, she clung to the rail, tears in her eyes. Hearing his voice inside her head as clearly as if he was standing right beside her.

I loved your mother so much then…still do if I'm honest. It broke my heart when she left me and I missed you both every single day. You mustn't blame her though; it was the fishing, you see. I was always going off in the boat, leaving her alone, worrying and wondering. I guess she just couldn't live with the sea…and I couldn't live without it—it's in my blood. Promise me, Ali, that you'll make sure I end up in the wildest ocean you can find. Scatter my ashes on the rolling sea and I'll be a very happy ghost.

They'd laughed about it at the time, but she *had* promised and she intended to keep that promise, no matter what. And this, she decided with a shiver of apprehension, must surely be about as wild as the sea could get.

The lights of the fishing boat penetrated the blackness of the night, bringing a shimmer to the rolling waves and outlining the dark bulk of the boat that suddenly lurched and heaved beneath her, knocking her off balance. She grabbed for the rail with one hand while turning her face into the wind, alarmed at its ferocity and yet totally intoxicated by the crashing of the waves and the salty tang of the ocean. She felt closer to her dad here than she had in the brief time she knew him, for this was his world. The sea had been his whole life and she owed it to him to make it his final resting place.

The wind howled menacingly in the cloudy black sky above and her apprehension gave way to real fear as the wooden deck seemed to suddenly disappear beneath her, thrusting her back up again as a mighty wave took the boat in its grasp. A wall of water towered above the cabin, crashing down onto the deck in a rushing mass of rippling white foam that almost took her feet from under her as she desperately clung to the urn with one hand and the rail with the other. The water forced her up against the side of the boat, but despite her looming awareness of the danger she was in, she kept her focus.

"I have to do this for you, Dad," she cried as the next wave rolled across the deck beneath her feet, knocking her off balance. The urn slipped from her fingers and she released the rail, dropping onto her hands and knees to make a grab for it.

"Ali! Ali!" Bobby's voice sounded distant against the howling wind. She glanced back for just a second and saw his bright young face beneath the waterproofs that hid his thatch of red hair. "Ali," he yelled again. "Hang on… I'm coming."

The boat leveled for a moment, and everything went strangely still. This was her chance. Seizing the opportunity, she grasped hold of the urn and unscrewed its lid, fighting back fear as she struggled to scatter the contents of the urn into the sea. The boat rolled violently as the next wave hit, and she hooked her fingers around the rail with a sense of relief. But as she upended the urn, the mighty wind whipped the gravelly dust and hurled it back in her face as if in mockery of her plight. Dust filled her eyes, her mouth. Panic seized her and for a moment everything froze. And then her fingers were slipping…slipping.

Bobby's voice rang in her ears. "Ali…! Ali… Hang on, I'm coming."

His words stalled as the next wave hit, lifting her off her feet. She fought for breath as it hurled her against the railing, tossing her like a rag doll up and over the side of the boat, down toward the raging black sea.

As she fell, Ali felt strangely distanced from the events overtaking her. Was this it then, the end? Was she to join her father in the roiling sea? Was that what he'd wanted?

"Ali!… Ali!" She heard Bobby's voice again, screaming in fear, but it was too far away.

Something suddenly grabbed her, stopping her fall midflight but almost tearing her arm from its socket. The icy water numbed her legs as she hung half in and half out of the ocean, gasping for breath as the boat sank down into the sea before lifting her out again to gulp in air. The noise overpowered her; the howl of the wind, the crash of the waves and all the time, in the background, the steady throb of *The Sea Hawk*'s engine. It felt like her heartbeat inside her head. She tried to move; a wave of agony ran down her arm and she started to scream. "Bobby... Bobby! Help me!"

CHAPTER TWO

IT WAS JUST as Bobby reached the hatch that Tom saw them. Ali was standing right by the rails, outlined against the formidable black sea by the boat's flickering light; her face was bright with a kind of raw exhilaration that took his breath away.

"Ali!" Bobby yelled, heading toward her. "Ali!"

Tom cursed silently. Didn't she realize just how dangerous her situation was?

"Ali!" Bobby yelled again, his voice now a scream that was whipped away by the howling wind. The boat rose on a wave, then dipped down suddenly. Ali lost her footing and the urn she was clutching fell from her hands onto the deck. "Leave it," Bobby cried.

Ignoring his plea she dropped down on her knees, reaching for the urn that was rolling across the wooden deck. Grabbing hold of it she turned to look across at Bobby, and Tom noted with a jolt of apprehension that the exhilaration in her eyes had now been replaced by raw fear.

"Hang on to the rail," Bobby yelled as the boat leveled out once more, but Ali determinedly began to unscrew the lid, trying to scatter the ashes into the sea as he made his way toward her. The wind whipped the contents of the urn into her face.

Tom saw the panic in her eyes as the storm took the boat back into its grip and for an endless moment time seemed suspended. The deck rose violently beneath their feet as another huge wave hit; Ali looked up in horror as the water towered above them, as high as the mast itself, before crashing down with a violence that stopped Tom in his tracks and forced Bobby back.

"Ali!… Ali!" his brother yelled again, his voice breaking as the wave hit her. In desperation she tried to hang on to the rail, fighting to stay on her feet as the powerful wave took her. Tom watched helplessly as she slid, over the side and into the raging sea.

"Bobby!" he screamed. His brother headed straight for the railing with no thought for his own safety.

Tom struggled along the rolling deck, watching the scene play out as if it was all happening to someone else. By now Bobby was leaning precariously over the rail, peering into the heaving ocean, the black water flickering and glistening in the yellow lights of the boat. He yelled Ali's name over and over, despite the roar of the wind.

To Tom's horror, he started to clamber over the rail… "I'm coming, Ali," he called. "Don't worry."

"Get back, Bobby," Tom shouted as another wave hit. He struggled toward the rail. "It's an order, Bob… Don't be stupid." His words were lost as the wave crashed down over the boat hurling him against the side.

Hearing the cries, the two other fishermen, Mike and their father, Jed, appeared on deck, struggling to balance against the force of the water as they went to help…but it was too late. By the time they joined Tom at the rail Bobby was gone.

Desperately scouring the heaving waves, an empty space where his heart should be, Tom detected a shape in the water. "There," he yelled. "Look!"

Mike peered down to where he pointed. "It's the girl." he said in a heavy tone.

"You get her," ordered Tom. "I'll keep looking for Bobby… Dad, can you get the floodlight out onto the sea and grab a life belt ready to throw out to him…and call Search and Rescue."

ALI FOUGHT TO stay conscious, fought to breathe, fought for her life against the raging sea as the icy cold water crashed over her again and again. A burning agony ran down her arm. She was stuck, caught up in something. All the while she could hear Bobby calling her name. His face was a blur as he looked down from the boat, the sea raining over him like a shimmering waterfall. And then he was a part of the waterfall, plummeting toward her. As the weight of his body thudded against her she tried to grab hold of him, clinging desperately onto his arm. For an endless second their eyes made contact and then he was gone, torn away by the cruel sea. Desolation hit and she closed her eyes, the whole world going black.

The pain made her cry out. It engulfed her, tearing through her shoulder and down her arm. Where was she? It was cold, so cold…

"Just hang on lass."

A deep masculine voice came from somewhere way above her. Was it God's voice she could hear? Reality hit as she felt herself being physically dragged upward and memories kicked in. "Bobby!" she called out, but her voice was just a croak.

"They're looking for him," came the man's voice again as he hauled her over the rails and onto the deck. Another wave of pain flooded over her but all she could see was the desperation in Bobby's eyes as she lost her grip on his arm. She should have tried harder. "It's Mike," the man said. "Remember me?"

"Mike," she repeated, recognizing the bearded face

that hovered over her. He picked her up as if she weighed nothing and carried her into the cabin, laying her down and removing her wet clothes with a sense of urgency but no embarrassment.

"Here," he said, wrapping her in a blanket and then in something shiny. "This will help keep your body temperature up…are you sure you're okay? You must be in shock."

She nodded urgently, fighting off dizziness and nausea. "Never mind me, I'm fine…go and help them find Bobby."

He didn't need asking twice. "Just stay here, inside," he told her, heading out again into the howling wind.

Ali watched from the window of the cabin, dragged down by misery and guilt. If Bobby… She fought back a sob, pressing her face against the window. If Bobby was lost it was all her fault. A spotlight flickered across the surface of the turbulent sea. The men peered over the rails, shouting his name over and over. "Bobby… Bobby… Bobby!"

At least he was wearing a life jacket she realized, so he couldn't drown…could he? And then she remembered something his brother Tom had said when he was sorting out some kit for her to wear on the boat, including a life jacket. She'd asked him if everyone had to wear one and his answer had surprised her. *"Not necessarily,"* he'd replied. *"In fact some fishermen won't wear life jackets at all because they think they're a waste of time. The thing is, though, if you do wear one then even if you drown, at least your body won't be lost at sea and your family will know for sure what happened to you."*

Her heart tightened as she remembered that moment. They'd laughed, she and Tom, as she tried on the huge oilskins, reminding her of when she'd been staying in his family's pub and they'd chatted in the bar about fishing and the sea. She'd thought they were friends, but he'd only reluctantly agreed to let her come on this trip, and apart from that one episode with the oilskins, he'd been curt and distant... Now she knew why. Her presence on the boat in such bad weather had put them all at risk.

Bobby couldn't drown, he mustn't drown... It wasn't right. And if he did...if he had, then it would all be down to her.

Hours passed, or what felt like hours to Ali. If only one of them would come and tell her something...unless there was nothing to tell. She nursed her arm to try and ease the pain, thinking about Bobby and feeling guilty for being warm and dry. Bobby was always so much fun, laughing, joking and singing karaoke in the pub. Someone so vibrant and bubbling with life had to be fine... didn't they? He was kind and caring, too, and so young. He had far too much left to give for his life to be taken; she just needed to stay positive.

Nursing her throbbing arm she cast her mind back to the first time they met. She'd gone with her husband, Jake, to a charity event at the college in Manchester where he lectured and Bobby was a student in his tourism and hospitality course. Jake introduced them and they'd chatted, just general stuff, but after that she'd seemed to keep bumping into him when she least expected it. They'd fallen into an unlikely and totally innocent friendship, and when her dad died and then her marriage went wrong and she'd had no one to talk to, he'd been there. In fact, she realized, she'd have been lost back then without his good advice and common sense.

You *need to take some time out*, he'd told her. *A trial separation to decide what you really want. Maybe you could even do something for your dad. You're a journal-*

*ist and he was a fisherman, perhaps you should write an
article on fishing and the sea, in his memory.*

His suggestion had taken root and grown. It had
seemed like such a good idea at the time, her coming to
stay at his family's pub, The Fisherman's Inn in Jenny
Brown's Bay, a little village between Arnside and More-
cambe. She'd so enjoyed talking to the fishermen who
frequented the pub in the evenings, especially Bobby's
older brother Tom and learning what her father's life must
have been like. In the end she'd taken a six month lease
on a cottage right down by the sea and begun writing her
article. She closed her eyes and shook her head…how had
it ended like this. If she hadn't taken Bobby up on his
suggestion to come here—or if she'd followed Tom's advice and stayed on shore—tonight would never have happened. Oh why did she always have to be so pigheaded?

Mike appeared again, peering cautiously round the
door. "You okay?"

She nodded. "Have you found him?"

"Search and Rescue are out looking." His mouth was
a grim line. "His brother Ned works for them and he's on
duty tonight so he'll find Bobby, I'm sure of it."

Ali saw the lights first, blazing through the blackness. She pressed her face against the glass. They must
have found him…

The Search and Rescue boat came right up against *The
Sea Hawk*, grating hull to hull. A man secured the ropes
and a familiar figure jumped effortlessly across the gap
between the boats… Ned, it was Ned.

He spoke to Jed first, placing an arm around his father's shoulders. When Jed dropped his face into his
hands Ali's heart sank and an unshed well of tears
stopped her breathing. No…no…no…this couldn't be
happening.

She was gasping for breath when Ned burst through the cabin door. "It's you…" he yelled. "My brother's dead because of you."

Ali sank to her knees, not noticing that the storm had died and the pale light of dawn was sneaking over the horizon, bringing the promise of a new day; a day that didn't have Bobby in it…because of her. "I am so, so sorry," she groaned, rocking from side to side, her pain forgotten.

"It's all your fault!" Ned said, turning away.

Eventually Tom came back to the cabin, his face ashen and his eyes dark and empty. Ignoring Ali he took the controls, piloting the boat on automatic. Half an hour went by before he spoke. "I told you to stay down below," he said without looking round. It was an accusation, Ali knew that, but she didn't know how to respond.

"Oh no. I'm sorry," she eventually managed, her voice little more than a whisper. Tom just stared ahead, and she could see his eyes were bright with tears he wouldn't allow himself to shed.

They traveled like that for over an hour, across the restless rippling sea, unaware of the glorious dawn that brought a hint of pale winter sunshine that made the water sparkle. It felt to Ali as if the sea was laughing at their plight, but still she couldn't hate it. She was the one who deserved to be hated. Mike came and went again, in silence, for there was nothing to be said.

Back at the harbor, Tom and Mike worked in silence, securing the boat. Ali sat motionless, still wrapped in a blanket, not knowing what to say or do. There was nothing she *could* do, no words she could say that might help. Her heart was a lump of lead inside her chest, her mind an empty space that was still trying to process what had happened. She looked at Tom… Bobby was his brother.

Tom just looked broken and lost.

A heavy flood of tears pressed against her eyelids. What she felt must be nothing to what he was going through. Bobby's death had been her fault, but she knew Tom would blame himself and he now had the task of going home with his dad to break the awful news to his mother, Grace, and his seventeen-year-old sister, Lily. They'd be waiting impatiently at The Fisherman's Inn right now, waiting for their family to come home…still unaware one of them was gone forever and the fishing trip that had started out as an adventure had become a nightmare that could never end.

Mike looked into the cabin as he was about to leave. "You okay?" he asked.

Afraid to see sympathy in his eyes when she didn't deserve it, she just nodded, unable to bring herself to look at him. "You need to go home now," he told her. "And try to get some sleep. I can give you a lift if you'd like."

She shook her head. "No need, thanks," she said, standing up and dropping her blanket onto the bench. "It's not very far. I'll be fine."

Tom was still on board when she left the boat and she watched and waited in the shadows until he locked the cabin, left the boat and walked woodenly across to his truck, looking neither left nor right. Only then did she start slowly walking et off toward her cottage on Cove Road, remembering how the adventure had begun, just yesterday. She'd walked so eagerly down to the boatyard, alight with excitement. And then she'd overheard them, Tom, Ned, Bobby and Jed, arguing about whether or not she should come along. Bobby had invited her and she'd been so looking forward to the chance to return her father's ashes to the sea. When she overheard Tom calling her a rookie and a city girl who'd cause only problems for them, she'd felt a rush of disappointment. It was Bobby who was her friend, but she thought she and Tom were building a friendship, too. He'd been so patient with her many questions and had given her a lot of information on fishing as a way of life. She'd been annoyed and maybe a little hurt to find out just how angry he was about Bobby inviting her along, especially when it was so important to her. Now she knew better. She dropped her face into her hands… Now she knew just how right Tom had been and just how foolish she was.

Opening the cottage door, she went through into the sitting room that overlooked the sea and collapsed on the sofa, feeling as if the whole world was closing in on her. Bobby Roberts was dead and it was all because of her.

CHAPTER THREE

ALI GROANED, clutching at her shoulder, her heart beating erratically as the memories kicked in… The boat… the sea…and Bobby; it was just a bad dream…had to be a bad dream. The agony in her arm said otherwise and she dragged herself up from her awkward position on the couch, crying out with the pain. She must have slept, but how could she, after everything?

Outside, bizarrely, the sun was shining, bringing a sparkle to the tranquil ocean, just as if it was an ordinary day. But it could never be ordinary again could it…not ever. Bobby was dead because of her and she had no right to be alive. Wracked by sobs she walked to the window, looking out at the scene that only yesterday she'd loved with a passion. Now it felt as if the sea was laughing at her, mocking her with its feigned serenity. A wave of dizziness washed over her and she shuddered. She needed to go to the hospital, she knew that, but it just felt so wrong. Why should she be free of pain when nothing could be done for Bobby?

Her car was parked outside. All she had to do was climb inside, put the key into the ignition, start the engine and drive herself to the hospital: a simple task that seemed almost impossible without the use of her right arm. *Almost*, she told herself determinedly, picking up her car keys with her left hand…

By the time Ali had managed to get into the driver's

seat she felt totally exhausted. Not only were her arm and shoulder screaming with objection, her whole body seemed to be rebelling. She felt sick and dizzy and her skin was rimed with cold sweat. Gritting her teeth she tried to put the key into the ignition with her left hand, wishing she'd done it before she got into her seat. When the keys dropped to the floor with a heavy jangling sound it all became too much. She slumped forward, giving way to a huge wave of dizziness, and rested her forehead heavily on the steering wheel.

She didn't know how long she'd been like that when she sensed a presence outside the car window. It might have been minutes or it might have been hours for she was in an empty place where time was lost in the weight of the past.

"Move over." She heard the voice somewhere in her subconscious, a man's voice, deep and familiar. A tingle of warmth crept through her veins as she turned awkwardly to see Tom standing by the door. "Move over," he repeated gruffly.

Soundlessly, she did as she was asked, gratefully making the transition from driver to passenger in a series of painful shunts. He opened the door and climbed in, sitting down heavily. His face was gaunt and set, staring soundlessly ahead. She wanted to say something, for him to say something, but a heavy cloud of silence settled over them. "Keys?" he eventually managed and when she gestured toward the floor he reached down and picked them up, putting them into the ignition and starting the engine.

The world outside the car was a fuzzy blur to Ali as they headed through the village and out onto the main road. Sea and sand and sky, buildings, cars and passersby, all became one intermingled image as the miles sped by. The hospital sign was the first thing she really saw.

Bright and bold it sprang out at her, offering comfort from the pain she so deserved… She glanced across to where Tom sat still, his expression unfathomable. Why had he helped her, she wondered, after…? And how had he known?

"Accident & Emergency is just there," he said, staring ahead as if unable to look at her.

She dragged herself from the car and headed for the double doors, leaning on the wall for support. And then he was beside her, taking her good arm and guiding her into the dazzling brightness. The woman at the desk looked up at them with a toothy smile. "Yes?" she said. "Can I have your name please?"

It was Tom who answered, his tone abrupt. "Her name is Ali Nicholas. She's hurt her arm."

"And you are…?"

"I just gave her a lift… I'll leave her with you now."

When he walked away without a backward glance Ali wanted to cry.

TOM DROVE ON AUTOMATIC, unable to process the events of the last twelve hours. His mother and younger sister, Lily, had taken the news badly and looked at him with accusation in their eyes. He was the one who was supposed to keep everyone safe and he'd failed. His instincts had warned him not to let Ali go out with them; he'd had enough warnings over the years. Why, just a year or so ago Ricky Biggins, an experienced fisherman and childhood friend of his, perished in a storm—fell from *The Peacock* and was never found. He should never have ignored his gut feeling and now it was too late…so if anyone was to blame it was he. Ali's failing was simply ignorance.

When his dad came home he'd placed a hand firmly

on his eldest son's shoulder. "It's fishing, son," he'd said.
"And sometimes there's a price we have to pay for what
we do… It's the sea that's at fault, not you."

Although kindly spoken, for Tom those words had
made things even worse. He didn't deserve pity or understanding, he'd failed his family, but most of all he'd
failed Bobby. "No, Dad," he'd said sadly. "I was in charge
and it should never have happened."

He'd walked away then from the oppressive silence
that hung thick and heavy in the large homely kitchen of
The Fisherman's Inn, through the locked and empty bar
and out into the impossible brightness of a late autumn
afternoon. There'd been nowhere to go then but home,
even though he already knew that his cozy cottage on
Cove Road couldn't provide any comfort this time.

He saw her sitting in her car as he walked toward his
cottage, just two doors down from hers. Ali! She was the
last person he needed to see. He'd tried to just walk past
the car where she sat so forlornly, looking determinedly
the other way…but when he heard a low moan he reluctantly peered inside. She was slumped forward over the
wheel, her skin the color of alabaster.

A vague recollection slid into his foggy brain. They
were searching for Bobby, scouring the surface of the
raging sea with increasing desperation, when Mike said
that he thought Ali might have dislocated her shoulder.
It had hardly registered…until that moment. He'd looked
again and knew he had to help her.

Unable to face the hospital where they'd brought
Bobby a few short hours ago, he'd intended to just drop
her off. But she'd walked so slowly toward the entrance,
holding on to the wall for support, that he hadn't been
able to simply leave her until she'd gone inside and seen

someone. As soon as the nurse came in he took his leave and fled.

He'd done what he could, he told himself as he'd driven away. She was in good hands, and if they released her she could easily ring a taxi. He needed to go home, to be on his own for a while to try and come to terms with what had happened. At the moment he felt as if he was living in a fog, a fog that held a nightmare he couldn't quite face up to.

He knew that he had to go back before he was hardly a mile away from town; it felt almost as if Bobby was there beside him telling him that he had to help her. She'd looked so shocked and gray and scared that despite what had happened, be it her fault or not, he couldn't just abandon her. With a lead weight in his heart he swung the car round in the road and headed back toward the hospital.

Mary, the A&E receptionist, told him to sit down while she went to find out what was happening. She came back after just a few minutes. "She's dislocated her shoulder and the doctor is with her now," she told him.

Tom couldn't muster a response. He showed no sign of interest or concern. He simply felt detached. The receptionist must have noticed because she peered at him closely and asked, "Are you okay?"

He nodded. "Yes…fine."

Mary smiled encouragingly, but Tom could see in her eyes that she was alarmed by the lack of expression on his face. "Don't worry, she won't be long now," she said.

THE DOCTORS HAD relocated and strapped her shoulder under anesthetic, and physically, Ali felt much better, but her head was in turmoil. She made her way back into reception with a packet holding prescription painkillers. When the nurse asked if she had someone to take her home and look after her she'd nodded. Bobby's death was still too raw for her to feel sorry for herself. She could manage on her own.

Now, though, she wasn't so sure; how was she going to get home? Feeling weepy and guilty and lost she stepped into the quiet waiting room where rows of people sat patiently...and there he was: Tom Roberts, waiting for her. With an almost imperceptible nod of his head he stood and she followed slowly in his wake, out into the red glow of the evening sun.

He drove slowly toward Jenny Brown's Bay, staring straight ahead. Ali knew he couldn't bring himself to look at her and she understood that. He pulled up on Cove Road, cut the car engine and climbed out. For a moment she thought he was just going to walk away but then, as if he'd thought better of it, he came round to her door to help her out. His hand on her arm felt cold and tight. "Thank you," she said but he didn't acknowledge her gratitude.

At the door he held out his hand. "Your key?"

She shook her head. "It's not locked."

The door opened with one push and she followed Tom into the kitchen, where he motioned to her to sit before walking across to fill the kettle at the sink. Neither of them spoke.

Ali nursed her arm, fighting off another wave of dizziness as the sound of the bubbling water gurgled inside her head. Tom just watched, grim-faced, as the steam rose in clouds, filling the room.

She wanted to reach out to him, wanted him to know how she felt. "I'm so sorry, Tom...so very, very sorry."

He brewed the tea and poured her a cup. When he handed it to her she saw that his eyes were dark with pain.

"Sympathy won't bring Bobby back," he said. "Nothing will."

He left then, abruptly, and she just sat for a while with her mind in turmoil. What now? She so wanted to help, to speak to Bobby's parents, to talk to Lily…and Ned. But what to say…what right had she to encroach on their grief?

FOR THE NEXT few days Ali hardly set foot outside. She watched Tom walk by the window every day from his cottage two doors down, staring straight ahead, his shoulders rounded. He never stopped though, never even gave her a glance or paused to ask her if she was okay. One day faded into another. She thought about Bobby, dwelled on if-onlys and remembered those pleasant evenings in the pub. She and Tom had chatted about fishing and life. She'd told him all about finding her dad just a few months earlier—that he'd been diagnosed with terminal cancer and how they'd finally gotten to know each other. She'd felt they were almost friends then, she and Tom. She'd even told him about her husband, Jake, not the details of course, just that they were having a trial separation. It had meant a lot to her, their friendship—he realized that now more than ever. But she knew that it could never be the same. Because of her, his brother, her good friend Bobby, was dead. How could either of them ever get past that? And yet he'd taken her to the hospital; she clung onto that thought like a lifeline.

It was late afternoon on the fourth day when a knock came at Ali's door, a knock so intense that it made the door frame rattle. Her heart leaped with hope but anticipation quickly gave way to dismay. Was it Tom? What would she say to him…?

She turned the handle just as the door burst open,

almost knocking her over. Stepping quickly back she braced herself against the wall as Ned Roberts appeared in front of her. His face was drawn, his eyes so black with an icy anger that she felt her whole body recoil.

"Happy are you?" he asked, his tone harsh, "Happy that you managed to survive when my brother died. We've been making the arrangements for Bobby's funeral today, you see, and all I could think of was you... living your life. He was just twenty years old with *his* whole life ahead of him and he's gone, snuffed out because of you."

Ali started to shake. "No... I didn't... I didn't mean it to happen. It was an accident, just an accident."

"An accident that wouldn't have happened if you'd stayed away from him. Bobby was almost ten years younger than you, little more than a boy, and yet you used his feelings for you to get what you wanted. You should never have gone out on the boat that night. You had no right."

"I'm sorry," she cried, her voice rising uncontrollably. "I'd do anything to make things different."

"Well, then, why don't you start by getting out of Jenny Brown's Bay and staying away from my family? No one wants you here."

With that parting shot Ned pushed past her and disappeared out the door. Ali sank to her knees, watching him run off along the shore. Ned was right, Bobby had been little more than boy and that was how she'd thought of him. To suggest that he'd had feelings for her and that she'd used him in any way was so far away from the truth. Closing her eyes tightly against the pain that flooded over her she rocked to and fro. She had to come to terms with this, had to try and understand what Ned was going through. He was just twenty five years old, six years younger than Tom, and he'd lost his baby brother because of her…he had every right to hate her. She'd so wanted to go to the funeral, to talk to Bobby's parents—and Tom—to help somehow, but maybe Ned was right and she should just leave.

After he'd gone she just sat there, going over and over that awful night, again and again. Ned's words circled round inside her head. *His life snuffed out, because of you…you lived and he died…no one wants you here.*

He was right, she realized, trying to pull herself together, everything he said was right. It had all been her fault, and she had no right to hang around sharing the family's grief. She'd come here, to Jenny Brown's Bay, with so many hopes and dreams, to finish with her old life and start afresh with new friends around her. Tom had been a friend but, like Ned, he probably hated her now. Not that she could blame him either. Everything had changed, so suddenly and drastically, that it was difficult to know what to think or what to do.

Time ticked by and still Ali sat, her mind a million miles away from the things that had seemed so important just days ago, like the article she was going to write. Her notepad lay unopened on the table and right now she didn't think that she would ever open it again.

When she heard the knocking at her door, her whole body froze. She couldn't face Ned's anger again however much she deserved it; there was nothing she could say to him that might help. When the knock sounded again, more urgent this time, she stumbled to her feet; what if it was someone else. Her hand shook as she reached for the door handle.

CHAPTER FOUR

TOM WALKED SLOWLY homeward along the clifftop, looking down at the stretch of silver sea that sparkled in the distance. Awaiting the returning tide, the wide sweep of sand shimmered, smooth and serene. In fact the whole scene looked so starkly beautiful and totally harmless right now that it seemed impossible to think that within just a couple of hours the sea would come rushing back in, tearing away the tranquility. That's what he'd always loved about the sea, its changeability. Now he was not so sure. It was in his blood though, an untamable beast that he couldn't resist, and he could never have a normal life because of it. What woman would want to share her life with constant fear and danger?

Someone moved way below him, across the sand, a tiny, sticklike figure in the distance. Ned, it was Ned. What was he doing…had he been to see Ali as he'd threatened to so many times? No, surely not, for no matter what his brother thought, there was no peace to be had from displays of anger or laying blame; he'd made Ned see that…hadn't he?

Increasing his pace he hurried along the clifftop path wondering if he should call in on her, just to make sure she was okay. He'd felt bad for ignoring her these last few days but everything had been too raw for him to be able to face up to the memories that seeing her might invoke. There was something about her that called out to him, a familiarity way deeper than their surface friendship; it had been forged when she was first at The Fisherman's Inn, when she'd picked his brains about being a fisherman... After Bobby's death, he found himself questioning his way of life. Fishing was in his blood, his soul, but was it worth the heartache it so often caused? Why, there were ten men he could name who had drowned over the last few years while following their life's passion, a passion that sometimes seemed cursed. *The Sea Hawk*'s fateful trip had been cursed, too, that night, cursed by love. For Bobby had been in love with Ali and he'd died trying to save her; how could any of them get past that? There could never be anything between Tom and Ali now that wasn't steeped in guilt, even friendship, because Bobby was no longer here. Tom needed time away from her, he knew that, time to grieve and time to sort out the confusion in his head.

Despite his determined thoughts as he approached her cottage, Number Three, his footsteps slowed again and doubt set in. She'd been so brave when he took her to the hospital. Her arm must have been in agony but she never even mentioned it. What if Ned really had called in on her; how must she be feeling? For a moment more he stood, indecisive, and then he slowly raised his hand to knock. When the door remained firmly closed, a flood of emotion overcame him, relief and disappointment vying for first place. He knocked again more firmly before suddenly reconsidering his actions. He couldn't do this. Turning sharply, he headed off into the night.

ALI PUSHED THE door open gently, peering through the crack into the falling darkness with a surge of relief; no one was there. She'd been so afraid that it was Ned again.

Her phone started ringing with the bright jubilant tone

that now sounded so wrong. She looked outside for a moment longer, just to reassure herself, before hurrying to answer it. The screen flashed with the caller's name— *Jake*—he was the last person she'd expected to hear from. For a moment she considered just ignoring it. She'd had her say before she left, about fidelity and promises…and yet, the urge to talk to someone outside of this nightmare was strong, someone who knew nothing of the tragedy.

"Hello," she said cautiously.

"Ali…where are you?"

She actually felt pleased to hear his voice and that was crazy after what they'd been through. "It doesn't matter where I am… Why are you ringing me?"

"To say sorry…again," he said. "Look, I know you don't trust me and I don't blame you, but I am still your husband… I know I hurt you and I don't deserve any forgiveness but I love you, Ali. I want us to try again and I really mean it this time… Please, Ali, come home…to talk, that's all, just talk."

Her first instinct was to cut him off, but something stopped her. After all, if she was honest with herself she knew that she craved forgiveness herself for what she'd caused, and here he was asking *her* for forgiveness for the damage he'd done to their relationship. She'd be a hypocrite if she didn't even listen to what he had to say. "I'll think about it," she promised.

"But where are you…you can tell me that at least?"

He sounded so genuine, so caring when she needed to feel cared for. "Jenny Brown's Bay," she told him, flicking off the phone.

Hearing Jake's voice brought back so many memories. They'd been in love once…until she found out that he'd cheated on her, and then love had slowly trickled out of the window. She'd tried to make a go of it, really tried…

until the next time. But he was right, he was still her husband, the man she'd promised to love for better or worse. A week ago she wouldn't have given him the time of day but now her priorities were all over the place. Take her dad for instance. She'd wanted to find him for almost all of her life but when she'd finally gotten her wish it was too late. Perhaps if her mother had been more forgiving, Ali would have had him in her life for a whole lot longer. She wanted, needed, forgiveness herself so perhaps the first thing *she* should do was to learn to forgive…or at least to listen.

By the time the pale winter sunshine crept through her window on the morning of the fifth day after Bobby's death, she'd made her decision. She wasn't wanted in Jenny Brown's Bay and she needed to get away, at least for a while. Going to see Jake and talk things through might help her focus on what she needed to do now. With trepidation she picked up her phone.

"Hello… Jake…?"

CHAPTER FIVE

ALI DUMPED HER bag by the door and looked around the cottage with a rush of regret. She'd come here with such a sense of purpose, hoping for a fresh start… Tears welled up but she pushed them aside; what right had she to cry when all she'd done was ruin the lives of the people who'd been so good to her. It had been Bobby's kindness that had put her on this path in the first place and now, because of her, he was no longer here… That put a whole new unpleasant light on everything. It hurt too, to think that Bobby may have had feelings for her, as Ned implied. If it was true then she'd really let him down because she should have realized; maybe she'd just been naïve but that was no excuse either. So was that was why he'd acted so rashly then, jumping overboard without thinking it through to try and rescue her. The thought that it might be true made her heart feel like lead in her chest.

She'd told Jake she'd be back in Manchester by early evening but now she was second-thinking her decision. It felt as if she was running away…but from what? No one wanted her here and no one wanted to hear her apologies for something that could never be undone. But was trying to rake up the ashes of the past really the right move?

Sitting down heavily on a kitchen chair she tried to sort things out inside her head but all she could see was Tom's face. What right did she have to even think about him? Their budding friendship had died along with

Bobby. No, she decided, the right thing to do was to keep away from the Roberts family and leave them to grieve in peace. Having her around would just be a grim reminder.

She heard the front door creak open as she gathered up the things she needed to take with her. "Hello!" she called, nerves tingling.

"Are you going somewhere?" Seventeen-year-old Lily Roberts stood in the hallway; her cornflower blue eyes open wide with surprise. "You will be back for Bobby's funeral though?"

"I…" began Ali. "Well."

Lily smiled gently, stepping forward to take hold of her hand with the typical naiveté that Ali found so refreshing. She'd met the slightly "different" member of the Roberts family on the very first night she'd stayed at The Fisherman's Inn, the pub and guest house Grace Roberts ran with help from the rest of the family, and they'd become friends at once. It was Tom who'd eventually explained why his sister was as she was.

Ali had been sitting in the bar with Tom, having one of the chats she had come to enjoy, when Lily, who lived and worked at home, approached to collect the glasses. "Are you going to fall in love with Tom?" she'd asked, looking at Ali with a childlike innocence.

Rather than being embarrassed or annoyed at his sister's outspoken question as Ali had expected, Tom just smiled indulgently, reaching across to pat her arm. "Lily always says it as it is," he said. "You'll get used to it… She's special, aren't you, Lil.'"

"Special," Lily repeated, her pretty face shining with delight, and Ali had thought in that moment that she did look special, kind of fey and otherworldly…like a fairy.

After she'd gone Tom went quiet, but then, as if suddenly coming to a decision, he put down his glass and

looked Ali straight in the eye. "Lily's birth was difficult—" he said slowly, twirling a beer mat between his
thumb and forefinger "—because the cord was around
her neck her brain was temporarily starved of oxygen. It
left her…different from other girls; she's beautiful and
kind and incredibly caring but she'll remain a child forever. We all have to look out for her."

He'd looked up at her then, his dark eyes soft with
emotion, and for Ali it had been a very special moment.
She could see that looking out for Lily was a huge responsibility, always would be, but she also knew without a doubt that he'd never shirk it. When he said that his
sister was special he meant it right from the heart. Tom
Roberts, she'd decided then, was someone you knew you
could always trust.

Seeing Lily here, at the cottage, was a painful reminder of that moment…of Tom. "Does anyone know
where you are?" she asked.

Lily shrugged. "Ned was shouting so I just walked
away. I don't like it when people shout. Do you shout?"

"I guess everyone shouts when they get cross or frustrated but some people shout louder than others."

"I don't think it was your fault that Bobby got drowned
anyway…do you have any biscuits?"

Ali handed her the cookie jar, a cold hand clamping
tightly around her heart. "Does everyone else think it
was my fault?"

"Ned does, that's why he was shouting."

"And Tom…does he blame me, too?"

Lily shrugged, nibbling her cookie, totally unaware of
just how much her answer meant. "Well I guess that everyone kind of blames you really because if you'd done as
Tom told you and stayed out of the way then you wouldn't

have fallen overboard and Bobby wouldn't have tried to save you."

When Ali's face fell, Lily smiled. "Don't worry," she said softly. "They know you didn't mean it. Mum says it was just a tragic accident and we shouldn't lay blame, so does Tom. It's Bobby's funeral soon—we're going to sing him to heaven. Please come."

"Oh Lily… I'm not sure that I'd be welcome."

"Bobby would have wanted you there… He liked you a lot."

For a moment Ali struggled to control a raw burst of emotion. "You really think so, Lily?" she eventually managed.

"I know so because he told me."

"What…what did he tell you?"

Lily's forehead puckered. "He told me not to say anything but I guess it doesn't matter now."

Reaching out, Ali took Lily's small, smooth white hands in hers. "Tell me, Lily…please."

"He said that he was falling in love with you but you didn't love him back yet…and anyway you were already married… Are you really married?"

Ali nodded. "We're having a break but…yes, I am still married."

"So why aren't you with your husband?"

At Lily's question, so innocently asked, Ali faltered, struggling for words. She wanted to be as honest as Lily herself but what should she say? "We had some problems," she eventually managed. "We are on a trial separation right now but we're going to meet up soon, to talk, you know, about the future."

"But you won't go until after Bobby's funeral?"

Lily's earnest expression tugged at Ali's heartstrings.

"I…" she began. "I mean… I'm not sure. Ned definitely won't want to see me there."

Lily shrugged. "We're all very sad… Mum says Ned is just lashing out… Please come."

"Do you think Tom will want me to be there?" she couldn't help asking.

Lily frowned. "I heard him say to Mum that he wished Bobby had never brought you here… But he did tell Ned that it was an accident and he mustn't blame you, and that you probably felt bad enough already… So you'll come?"

"I'll think about it," Ali promised. "Now you'd better get off home before someone comes to look for you. They'll be worried."

As she watched Lily head off down Cove Road Ali wondered if perhaps she should ring the pub, just in case they *were* looking for her. Before she could go and get her phone she saw Lily waving excitedly at someone. Tom—it was Tom. Lily pointed back toward the cottage, gesticulating wildly, and Tom followed her gaze. When, just for a fleeting moment their eyes met and held across the distance, Ali's heart skipped a beat. If only they'd met in another time and place, she thought with a lurch of regret, how different things between them might have been.

LILY WAS SO pleased to see Tom. "Hi, Tom," she called, flicking her blond braids back over her shoulders. "I've been to see Ali."

Tom stopped in his tracks, looking toward the row of cottages. "But why would you do that, Lily?" he asked. "And you know you're supposed to let us know where you're going?"

"There's Ali," cried Lily, ignoring him. "Look, she's over there, outside her cottage."

Tom followed her gaze to where Ali stood watching

them. She looked lost, he thought with a surge of guilt, and so alone. Perhaps he should have checked on her, just to make sure she was okay. When their eyes met across the distance a heavy sadness turned his limbs to lead. Should he go and talk to her?

No, he decided, it was just too complicated right now; he needed to stay strong for the family and being close to her might cloud his judgment. In fact it really would be easier for everyone if she just went back to where she came from…deep down though, in his heart of hearts, he knew that he longed for her to stay.

"She's going away soon," Lily said, as if reading his mind. "I told her she had to stay for the funeral though."

"Now why would you do that, Lil?" he asked. "You know Ned won't want her there."

"And you, do you want her there? Bobby would and you know it."

"Oh Lily, life is not quite as simple as you think. We'd all be better off without her around."

Lily stopped in her tracks, a flood of color turning her pale skin a creamy rose. "I wouldn't…" she said. "And I don't think you would either."

"And where's she going anyway? She's taken the cottage for six months."

"To see her husband I think, they're having a…a trial…separation."

"Well…that's it then," Tom said, turning determinedly on his heel. "She's leaving anyway. Come on, let's go home, everyone's worried sick about you."

WATCHING THEM WALK away together, brother and sister, so close, made Ali aware of just how lonely she was. The dad she'd found too late was gone, following her mother who'd died well over a year ago. So who did she have to care about her... Jake? He wanted to give their marriage another try, but look what he'd done to her before... and had he *really* changed? Did anyone really change? She'd told him she'd be there tonight but she just wasn't ready yet.

Picking up her phone she scrolled down to his number, taking a deep breath. "Sorry Jake," she told his voicemail. "I'm not going to be able to make it after all."

He rang back almost immediately. "What is it, Ali? Why would you want to stay in that godforsaken spot anyway? I get that you wanted to get away but it's time to come back to reality now. You're my wife and we belong together."

"No, Jake," she said, sure now that she was doing the right thing. "We don't belong together anymore, maybe we never did. We're over—were over the moment you lied and cheated..."

The sound of him slamming down the phone confirmed her intention. Jake would never change.

CHAPTER SIX

TOM WOKE BEFORE 6:00 a.m. feeling like he hadn't slept at all; sleep didn't come easy, he realized, when you were burying your brother the following day. He lay in his bed listening to the muffled sounds; thumping, bumping and gurgling water; people getting ready for the day ahead. Seemingly no one had slept easy.

The whole family had stayed at home in the pub, just like the old days. Far from bringing them all together as a family, however, it had just seemed to scream out the fact that Bobby was no longer there. His mother had insisted that they eat together, as they'd always done when they were kids. She'd even set Bobby's place at the table and that had been tough.

It was Lily who'd lightened the mood with her usual straightforwardness. "Bobby would have hated this," she declared at the dinner table. "Tomorrow we are going to sing him goodbye and he wouldn't want us to be sad… so come on, let's sing now."

And they had; all of them. They'd sat and sang some of the fishing songs Bobby loved, songs that were a part of the heritage Tom felt had turned against them. He'd found it hard to listen to the words for he couldn't help but question everything about his existence right now. After they sang, though, they'd talked, really talked, about Bobby, sharing wonderful memories that really meant something; and it had brought a smile back to his mother's face. She'd made them all promise there and then that tomorrow they would celebrate Bobby's life and not grieve for his death.

It had seemed so easy a promise to make, but in the gray light of dawn, things felt much different. Still, tomorrow, Tom decided, despite his apprehension, he was going to go fishing again; hopefully Bobby would be with him in spirit and help him to sort out his head.

After a reluctantly eaten family breakfast cooked by his mum, Tom headed back to his cottage by the sea on the pretext that he needed to change; the truth was he needed some solitude to get a grip on things. His steps slowed as he walked past Number Three; was Ali home he wondered? He couldn't see her car. Or had she already gone back to her husband. No matter, she was long gone from his life and that was a good thing…wasn't it? It had to be, nothing more to it.

ALI WAS DRIVING through the village. She passed by so many people, some somberly dressed in black but others making a statement by wearing bright colors to celebrate Bobby's life. She liked that, she decided, slowing down to let a group of young men in their fishing gear cross the road.

On a whim she pulled over near the village green and parked her car at the side of the road just down from the church. No matter what anyone thought, she decided, she needed to be here.

At eleven forty-five the gathered crowd began filing into the small stone country church. She got out of her car and joined them, slipping in at the very back, head down and hands trembling. A sob caught in her throat as she thought about Bobby, and then she remembered what Lily said. *We're going to sing him to heaven. Will you come?*

"Yes, Lily," she murmured. "I will come."

"You all right dear?" asked the elderly woman on her right.

Ali nodded dumbly, guilt washing over her; she had no right to be there.

The woman placed a hand on her arm. "It's good that you came," she said, a smile lighting up her worn features. "Accidents happen all too often, especially in fishing, and retrospect is just a waste of time. Life's too short for if-onlys... I should know that. Anyway, it's brave of you to show your face."

"Thanks," Ali said. "I realize that everyone around here knows I was on the boat when it happened and I thought everyone would be against me... so your support really means a lot. I'm not brave though. I just had to come because I owe it to Bobby...to say goodbye."

"Well I'm sure he appreciates it... In fact, who knows, perhaps he's watching us right now."

"Do you really believe that?" Ali asked.

Her question was drowned out by the ripple of music that announced the family's arrival and the entire congregation peered around discreetly. Four members of Search and Rescue, including Ned, carried the gleaming oak coffin on their shoulders, and behind them, walking slowly, his gray head bowed, was Jed Roberts; his wife leaned heavily on his arm, her face pale and drawn.

It was Tom, though, who took Ali's attention. He looked straight ahead, his jaw set and his eyes dark with emotion as he held on tightly to his sister's arm. True to her word, determined to make it a celebration, Lily wore a beautiful pale blue dress and had flowers in her hair. Holding her slender form as tall as she could she walked determinedly next to Tom, swaying slightly; her delicate features held an ethereal quality, as if she were one of the angels in the stained-glass windows.

When the family group were almost at the front of the church, Lily turned and peered inquisitively around her. Her gaze fell on Ali and she gave her a dazzling smile of welcome.

"Now that little lass has the right idea," murmured Ali's companion. "She's celebrating his life."

A myriad of emotions flooded the church as the beautiful service unfolded, especially when Tom and Ned stood up together at the front and talked from the heart about Bobby, bringing him back to life with recollections of their childhood, growing up in Jenny Brown's Bay. Their memories swung from moving moments to floods of hilarity. As the congregation laughed and cried as one, somehow it helped. The hymns and songs the family had chosen were beautiful, ranging from "All Things Bright and Beautiful" to one of Bobby's favorites, a bawdy fishing song. Ali joined in with the others, singing her heart out, and felt somehow cleansed. Bobby wouldn't lay blame; that was one thing she was sure of.

When the service drew to a close, a profound silence filled the church, just before the family slowly filed out after the coffin. Tom looked so regal in his dark suit, so strikingly handsome and so very, very sad that Ali longed to just go to him and offer...what? He looked up as he passed her and caught her eye, holding her gaze as if expecting to find something there. Emotion flickered in his dark eyes and her whole body trembled; she couldn't stay here, in Jenny Brown's Bay, even if she wanted to, for she'd be a constant reminder to the Robert's family, a knife in their wound.

When she watched him walk by, tall and straight and

so…honest, she felt lost and alone. Being close to Tom was unbearable, for if she was honest with herself she knew that she wanted way more from him than he could give, and she had no right to anything.

Straight to the point as usual Lily had asked her outright why, if she was still married, she wasn't with the husband.

And she realized Lily was right. So perhaps it was she who was lacking. Maybe she just wasn't the kind of woman who could ever maintain a real relationship. She should focus on her career now. That's what she needed to do. Journalism had meant everything to her once, after all.

Then she'd met her dad again and realized just how important family really was and how empty her life had become. Even her marriage had been almost a convenience that fit in around both she and Jake's careers; perhaps that was why it had gone so wrong. Meeting and getting to know her dad had made her realize what she'd missed, made her see that if only her mum had been less bitter things could have been so different. Now it was time for her to back track and rethink everything.

Walking slowly out of the church without looking back, she cut along the edge of the graveyard and headed toward her car, trying to think of anything other than Bobby and Tom and all the pain she'd caused.

As she opened the driver's door she sensed someone behind her.

"Ali…" came Lily's voice. "Don't go."

With a heavy sigh she turned to see Tom's sister standing forlorn in her beautiful dress.

"Your singing was beautiful, Lily," she said. "You did Bobby proud."

Lily beamed at her. "Thank you. Please don't go."

Ali shook her head slowly. "I have to, Lily. I'm in the way here."

"But you will come back?"

Ali gave her a hug, holding her close. "I'll try, Lily, I really will try."

CHAPTER SEVEN

TOM WASN'T SURE exactly why he felt so empty inside when he saw Lily saying goodbye to Ali. After every-thing that had happened he should be glad to see the back of her, angry even that she'd dared to stick around.

When Ali held out her arms, hugging Lily close, Tom let out a sigh. She was wrong for him for so many rea-sons, quite apart from the stark fact that she'd caused his brother's death. Anyway, there was no place in his life for a relationship right now Bobby drowning at sea had substantiated that fact. A fisherman's life was way too unreliable and dangerous to expect any woman to share it.

It was good that Ali was leaving. Being around her held way too many complications... So why then did he still feel a sense of loss? There was just something about her he supposed...the way she held her head...the way her eyes crinkled at the corners when she smiled, and her intensity. Never had he met a woman so resolute about what she wanted...like the way she'd insisted on joining their ill-fated fishing trip. Her warm brown eyes had flashed with streaks of flame when they'd had their disagreement about that. Oh how he wished now he'd tried harder to stop her.

There again, he decided, maybe things happened for a reason and that was just how it was meant to be... Fate, he supposed it was. Something deep inside him wished that fate would bring her back one day. Common sense told him to be glad she was leaving.

IT WAS STRANGE to be driving through the city again, thought Ali. Car horns honking, people scurrying by, pale distant faces. Life was just so different in the country, particularly by the sea where the rhythm of the tide seemed to take over everything.

The town hall clock began to chime, shaking her from her reverie, one…two…three…four…five. She'd booked a hotel for a few days, close to the city center and the offices of the paper where she worked…or used to. Being self-employed she'd traveled around a lot but *The Times* had given her most of her work and Jason, the editor and her longtime friend, had been only too pleased to have a meeting with her when she'd rung him earlier. Nosing her way through the traffic she eventually found a parking place and with a relieved sigh she pulled her bags out of the trunk, locked her car and headed for her hotel. It was good to be back in the city, she told herself determinedly as she unlocked the door of her room and collapsed on the bed; hopefully being so far from Jenny Brown's Bay would help her see her situation more clearly.

She ordered sandwiches in her room for dinner and went to bed early hoping that at last she might be able to get a good night's sleep. Beyond her window the flickering lights and bustling sounds of the street made that impossible. She tossed and turned, longing for the gentle swish of the sea or even the moaning cry of the wind.

Jenny Brown's Bay did seem like a million miles away, distancing her from the horror she'd left behind there. But was this really the answer, she asked herself, the way to get past what had happened…or was she just hiding from it? One thing she did know was that she missed the peace and tranquility of her cottage…missed it with an aching loneliness.

Ali finally gave up on trying to sleep at around five thirty and quickly washed and dressed, heading out into the city. Homeless people were waking up in doorways and under bridges, getting ready to face another day of struggling to survive. When she'd lived in the city she hadn't really taken much notice of the early morning activity, now she found it sobering.

A young lad with lank greasy hair and shadows under his eyes crept up to her, holding out his hand. "Give us a break miss," he said, his voice thin and reedy.

Ali delved into her purse and pulled out a handful of notes. "Promise me you won't spend it on drugs," she said.

"Don't do drugs," responded the boy. "Thanks miss. This money'll get me back home."

Feeling good about helping him Ali headed back to the hotel to get ready for her meeting with Jason. Maybe things would look up, she decided, as she showered and changed; maybe this was a new start.

By ten thirty she was out in the street again, dressed in a smart navy suit and heels; her shoes tip-tapped along the pavement as she headed toward the café where she was meeting Jason for coffee and a chat. She felt businesslike and professional, just like she used to before her priorities changed.

She saw the boy as she hurried across the street when the lights switched. He was just a blur in the corner of her eye but it was definitely him, handing money to a shifty looking man who passed him something in return. When she looked back they'd gone but she knew it had been the homeless lad from early that morning.

Stopping in the midst of the hustle and bustle of the street she shuddered deep inside, her freshly restored confidence draining away. All she'd done with her misplaced sense of benevolence was to push the lad more quickly down the road to nowhere. Now he could buy his drugs and maybe even die in a gutter tonight…so perhaps she'd killed him, too.

Ali didn't hear Jason calling her name until he was standing right in front of her, tall and solid and comfortably familiar; they went back a long way, she and Jason, both as work colleagues and friends. "Ali," he cried. "You were miles away and you look as if you've seen a ghost…come on, I'll buy you that coffee and you can tell me all about it."

Ali sipped her cappuccino slowly, still trying to process what she'd seen.

"So…" Jake asked. "Are you going to tell me what's up or is this purely business?"

Putting down her cup she looked up at him, smiling. "Sorry…right now it was about me taking pity on a homeless boy this morning and giving him way too much money. I just saw him now though, down a side street, obviously buying drugs, and it sickened me… I thought I was helping but I've probably just made his situation worse. What if he ODs and it's my fault?"

Jason laughed. "Oh Ali you really have been out of the city for too long. You can't help people like that. They're on a road to destruction I'm afraid. I see it every day when I'm driving home."

"But he's someone's son," Ali cried. "And surely everyone deserves to have some help."

"When you put it like that," Jason responded. "I guess they do. Anyone's kid can go down the wrong road I suppose… But there's more to it than that, isn't there, Ali.

Look, we're friends aren't we? Tell me what's been happening to you first and then we can discuss work."

Ali shook her head slowly. The thought of unburdening herself to someone outside of the tragedy in Jenny Brown's Bay was so tempting…and yet. "It's my problem, Jason," she said. "I'm here to see if you have any work for me…that's all."

Jason folded his arms across his chest, stroking his neat brown beard. "I have plenty of time today and as I just said…we can discuss work when we've talked about you. We go back a long way, Ali, why, you knew me before I was a hotshot editor."

"Well you're certainly that now," Ali remarked, lightening the mood.

Jason grinned. "And proud of it, too. Anyway, back to you… I want to help and so would Laura if she was here. Look how you were there for us and the kids when our house got flooded, not to mention all the other times. I'm not taking no for an answer I'm afraid. I'll go get us another coffee and then you can tell me all about it."

By the time Jason came back with the coffees he'd obviously given his approach some thought. Sitting down opposite her he looked Ali in the eye.

"Why don't you tell me about your dad first," he suggested. "Last time I saw you you'd just met up with him again as I remember…"

"He died," she blurted out and suddenly the floodgates opened. "Sorry…it's all still a bit raw. He was ill when I found him you see…with cancer. He lived alone in a little fishing village in the northeast; he had friends to help him of course but no one close. We talked, a lot, about his life and why Mum left with me when I was small, but he didn't bear a grudge. In fact he was sorry to hear that she'd died and he blamed himself for her leaving him all those years ago. I really got to know him in those last few weeks and I came to understand something of the fisherman's passion for the sea—it's a way of life, a vocation, I suppose, and it causes rifts in so many marriages. He loved it though to his dying day and he opened my eyes to the magnificence of the sea…that's why I ended up at Jenny Brown's Bay."

"Jenny Brown's Bay," Jason repeated slowly. "Is that a fishing town then?"

Ali nodded. "It's just a village really. I still have a cottage rented there. Jake and I split you see…"

"Well I'm not surprised at that," Jason cut in. "Never did like the guy."

"But you only ever met him a couple of times."

"Two times too many then. You're well rid of him."

"I've come to realize that," said Ali sadly. "Anyway, I was still cut up about my dad when Bobby, a student of Jake's who I'd gotten to know, suggested I stay at his parents' pub for a while. I'd decided to write an article on fishing, in memory of my dad. He thought I could do some research there."

"And did you?"

"Oh yes," she nodded eagerly, remembering. "I used to have long chats with Bobby's brother Tom, he was passionate about fishing just like Dad…in fact all Bobby's family were. And I talked to some of the old fishermen, too, they used to come to the pub in the evenings. I learned a lot from them…except perhaps about the danger."

Jason leaned toward her, speaking in a gentle tone. "So what happened there?" he asked. "Obviously it was something traumatic…or is this all just about your dad?"

For a moment Ali went quiet. "In a way it's about

Dad," she began, struggling to keep her voice steady. "But there's more."

Jason waited for her to go on, saying nothing.

"Bobby suggested I go on a night fishing trip with him and his brothers, you know, for my research. Tom was dead against it...they had a row. He said he wasn't prepared to take a rookie on a night trip, especially a woman, as it was far too dangerous. You know me, I was furious and, bottom line, he gave in and said that although he didn't approve, since his father, Jed, didn't seem to mind, I could go along. After he'd agreed, in fact, he found me some waterproofs and gave me advice about the trip... I was so looking forward to it—it was important to my dad that I scatter his ashes in the sea."

"And I'm guessing it went wrong," Jason said.

Ali looked at him ashen-faced. "There was a storm, Bobby drowned and it was all my fault. I took a stupid risk, didn't listen to orders. When I went overboard he jumped in to save me..."

He reached across to place a sympathetic hand on her arm. "Accidents happen, Ali...you can't take all the blame."

"I can this time," she said quietly.

"You must have liked it there if you rented a cottage," Jake said "You should go back...face your demons I suppose you could call it."

Ali nodded. "I've thought about it. I was considering writing a book instead of just an article, and maybe make it about Bobby. I could still dedicate it to Dad, too."

"It's a lovely idea," Jason agreed. "Tell you what, why don't you come and stay with us for a couple of days. Laura would love to have a chat with you and the kids will cheer you up and bring you down to earth. Then you can decide whether to come to work at *The Times* or go back to your fishing village and write."

"Deal," Ali cried, holding out her hand to shake his. "And Jason…"

"Yes?"

"Thanks."

With a broad grin he pulled his cell phone from his pocket. "I'll ring Laura right now," he said. "She'll be over the moon…and Ali…"

"Yes?"

"If you do decide to stay and work here for a while then you're welcome to our spare room you know."

"I might just take you up on that. It will give me time to get my head straight and let things settle down a bit before I go back to Jenny Brown's Bay."

"Or not?" Jason responded.

Ali shrugged. "Who knows."

CHAPTER EIGHT

THE SEA WAS already rough when the boat set out across the bay in the crisp light of dawn. "Are you sure about this?" Ned called above the chugging of the engine.

Tom looked up at the rolling gray clouds; ice-cold spray splattered across his face and gulls screamed overhead as *The Sea Hawk* cut through the waves. "What do you think?" he responded, looking across at his brother.

"That we should have done it sooner."

"Then let's go fishing," Tom cried, feeling more alive than he had since they set off on that fateful fishing trip. Deep down he'd been dreading going back out onto the water but now he realized he'd been wrong to delay it, for the ocean still felt like home, just as it always had before.

As if trying to make up for the tragedy it had caused, the sea was abundant with its offerings. When they got to the fishing ground both men worked hard and fast, hauling in cod after cod, delighting in the job they loved and exhilarated to be back out on the open waves.

It wasn't until he started to steer the heavily stocked boat back toward Jenny Brown's Bay that Tom's mind rewound to that last fishing trip. He'd been on automatic since the accident, he could see that now, trying not to allow himself to think or feel, just getting on with what had to be done in the best way he could. Bobby's death had aged his parents, to survive a son held a terrible guilt, he guessed, so it felt as if he had to step up and take responsibility for the whole family. A rush of sorrow dulled the triumph of today's catch as his eyes fell on the rolling waves ahead; he'd been determined to stay strong for everyone but now, back in what felt like normality again, he felt suddenly drained.

"You okay, Tom?" Ned asked, peering at his older brother with concern.

Tom felt himself wilt and leaned forward over the wheel. "Just tired I guess."

"Go and have a lie-down," Ned urged, taking the wheel. "I can get this little lady home no problem."

"You sure?" To Tom the idea of just letting go for a while seemed very appealing.

Ned grinned. "Hey… You can count on me. I'm with Search and Rescue you know."

Stepping back Tom slapped him gratefully on the shoulder. "So you are. Have I ever told you how proud I am of that?"

Ned's smile suddenly faded as memories kicked in. "Couldn't save Bobby though could I?"

"Not your fault," Tom insisted. "No one could have saved him."

"She could—" Ned blurted out "—by staying away from us."

For a moment Tom just looked at him, a rush of protectiveness for Ali bringing a heavy lump into his chest. "It was just circumstance, Ned…" he said slowly. "Fate. You can't lay blame like that. I'm sure she's as sorry about it as anyone."

"Sorry she may be but she's torn this family apart. And where is she now…back in her husband's arms I'm guessing. Well I sure hope she's not happy."

"Bitterness only hurts the bearer," Tom said quietly. "You have to let go of it, Ned, or it'll tear you up."

Ned's knuckles turned white as he held on to the wheel. "I think I'm prepared to take that chance. Now you go below and get some rest before I change my mind… and, Tom?"

"Yes…"

"She's nothing but trouble so stop defending her."

Remembering the pain in Ali's honey-brown eyes Tom was not so sure he could do that. Resisting the urge to say anything more, he just raised his hand; it didn't really matter anyway because she was gone and he didn't think there was much likelihood of her ever coming back.

ALI WAITED NERVOUSLY inside the busy pub where Jake had agreed to meet her. It was Laura who'd persuaded her to go. "You need to sort it out once and for all," she insisted. "Tell him that it's over and you want a divorce."

Jason had backed her up. "Laura's right you know, Ali. I've told you over and over that you need to put your life straight. You can't move on until you've finished with the past."

"But I'm not sure where I want to move on to," she'd told them. "I love my work but obviously I can't stay with you indefinitely… I mean, it's been great and I really appreciate you having me but you don't want a lodger forever…"

"You can stay as long as you like," Laura had insisted. "Can't she, Jason?"

"Of course," he agreed, looking intently at Ali. "But I don't think she really wants to."

"Then what do you think I want, Jason?" Ali asked. "Because I sure don't know… I mean, well I've loved working with you these last few weeks but…"

"You need to go back to your cottage by the sea and sort your head out," he told her with no hesitation.

"Yes," agreed Laura. "Jason's right. It's obvious that Jenny Brown's Bay is where your heart lies…there's too much emotion there for you to switch it off without facing up to what happened, and it's the only place where you'll find out what you really do want from your life."

"If money's the problem you can do some work for the paper from there," suggested Jason.

Feeling suddenly emotional at the generosity of her friends, Ali gulped back tears. "Sorry," she said, rubbing her eyes. "And thanks, Jason, for that offer but, to be honest, my dad left enough funds for me to take some time out…that's why I was going to write the article."

"Then make it a book," he urged. "For the young man who drowned and for all the other fishermen, too…like your dad."

Ali went quiet, drawn by the suggestion but so unsure. "I've still got some work to do for the paper though."

"Well finish that first then," cut in Laura. "And anyway it's only a few weeks to Christmas and we wouldn't enjoy it if we thought you were all on your own. Stay with us for that at least, we insist, but then I do agree with Jake that you need to go back and face all that heartache and emotion you left behind, it's the only way to get past it. You need to sort things out with Jake first though…"

"Thanks for the kind offer of Christmas." Ali said. "I really appreciate it…and after that we'll see. The trouble is that I've never actually written a book, what if its rubbish?"

"It won't be," Jason insisted. "Your writing's first class—all you need to do is get all the information you can and then listen to your heart."

Now, sitting in a bar sipping a glass of wine as she waited for her ex to appear, Ali thought about that conversation for what felt like the millionth time; since Jason and Laura had determinedly planted the idea in her head she'd become more and more drawn to the idea of writing a book for Bobby, her dad and all the other fishermen. Now, finally, the work she'd been doing for Jason was finished and on Laura's strict orders she'd taken the plunge and rung Jake. Their marriage was over, she'd never been more sure of anything, and today she was going to tell him straight.

With Jason's confidence in her journalistic competence buoying her, the idea of writing the book began to consume Ali; it felt like a need, a way to try and put things straight…or as straight as they could ever be. She'd even contacted Elsa May Malone Evans, the owner of her cottage, to arrange another six months' lease so that she didn't lose the option of going back to live there. Seeing Jake today felt like the last piece of the puzzle and she hoped that when it was slotted into place she would know what to do with her life.

She'd felt so certain about her meeting with Jake, but now that the moment was here, apprehension flooded over her. Whatever was she going to say to the man she'd lived with for almost three years, the man she'd sworn to love forever; that promise seemed like nonsense now, and she silently vowed to never give herself so wholeheartedly again. The failure of this marriage made a mockery of love and that was sad.

As she saw him appear along the street, however, dapper and stylish, sure of himself and full of self-confidence, her apprehension faded. How could she have ever believed that he was the man for her, she wondered, remembering Tom's tough, quiet approach to a life that was driven by his passion for the sea? Putting Jake straight about ending their marriage no longer seemed like a problem, more just a means to an end.

He approached across the busy bar carrying a pint of beer and sat, giving her his best, well-practiced smile. "So," he said, taking a gulp of the amber liquid. "You've finally seen sense."

"Hello, Jake," she said. "And yes, you're right—I have come to my senses. I just came to meet you so that I could tell you face-to-face. I'm filing for divorce and I'll be coming for the rest of my things tomorrow. Whatever we had is long gone, Jake. I wish you happiness and a successful future but it won't be with me."

CHAPTER NINE

BIT BY BIT in Jenny Brown's Bay a slow healing began. Just two weeks after Tom and Ned braved the sea again Jed Roberts finally decided it was time he, too, faced his demons and went out with his two sons on a fishing trip. No one mentioned Bobby's name as they headed out into the English Channel but in every one of the familiar tasks they undertook he was there.

It felt good, thought Tom, to feel Bobby's presence around them without that first deep cut of agony. The pain of his loss would be with them forever but the happy memories of his young brother could only bring joy.

"He'll always be with us won't he," Jed said, looking across at his sons as they made their way homeward.

"Sure will," Tom agreed. "In fact he's probably laughing at our long faces right now."

"He'll no doubt be bringing laughter to heaven," Jed added.

"He should be here with us," cut in Ned, his face dark with anger. "It should never have happened."

"But it did," Jed told him sadly. "And bitterness will only bring more pain. You have to let go, son, for your own peace of mind—even your mother is trying to move on and it's cut her deeper than any of us."

AS HER HUSBAND and two remaining sons began to re-kindle their love affair with the sea and let go of their fears, back home Grace Roberts had finally persuaded herself that it was time to go through Bobby's things and allow him to rest. Standing in the doorway to his room she fondly remembered how he'd always clung on to his childhood belongings, like Podge, the well-worn yellow bear who sat on a shelf with other keepsakes. His brothers had teased him about keeping Podge but Bobby hadn't cared. In fact, Grace realized, life in general had rather slid right over him; nothing ever bothered Bobby much. It was a part of having older brothers she supposed, teasing him and trying to wind him up but always there as a backup when needed.

Tears filled her eyes as she held the scruffy little bear close. She'd give it to Lily, she decided. She'd take good care of it and Bobby would have loved his little sister to have it. Her eyes fell on the items she had carefully placed on the dressing table, just as if they were waiting for him to pick them up. The baseball cap he always wore, with a comical fish on the front, his diary and his cell phone. She picked up the phone, its screen black. Emotion flooded over her as she grabbed the charger. She'd give the phone to Lily, too, bring it back to life again.

Holding tight on to the precious items she left the room, gently closing the door behind her. She'd made a start and that was enough for one day.

Lily was in her room, just down the corridor from Bobby's. With her usual astute awareness, she went to the door. "I'm glad you've been to Bobby's room at last, Mum," she said. "He wouldn't have wanted you to stay away."

Grace placed her arm about her daughter's shoulders and gave her a quick hug. "I know, love. I should have faced up to it sooner but… I just… I'm sorry."

"You don't have to say sorry to me, Mum. Bobby

would understand, too, so you don't ever need to say sorry to him."

"Your dad told me that you often go and sit in Bobby's room, I think that's what made me realize that it was time I stopped hiding."

"And did it help? It helps me, kind of makes me feel as if he's still there. I talk to him and I'm sure he can hear me."

Grace pressed her lips against the pale gold of Lily's hair. "Do you know, Lil, it's been well over two months?"

"Sometimes it seems ages since Bobby died and Ali went away," Lily said. "And sometimes it seems like yesterday."

Grace nodded. "You liked her, didn't you?"

Lily shrugged. "She was my friend…what are you doing with Podge?"

With a smile Grace held the teddy bear up as if it was talking to Lily. "I want you to look after me please," she said in a high-pitched voice.

Lily laughed, reaching out for the bear and cradling it in her arms. "Of course I'll look after you, Podge. You can even sleep in my bed."

"There's something else, too," Grace went on. "I think Bobby would want you to have his phone… Here."

When she handed it over Lily's face lit up. "Honestly…?" she cried. "And I really can use it and everything?"

"You really can use it and everything," Grace told her, feeling pleased with her decision. "I suppose you could think of it as your Christmas present from Bobby. Now here's the charger so why don't you go and plug it in right away. I'm off to get on with lunches. Perhaps you could come down and help me in a bit…when you've had a play with the phone."

LEFT ALONE IN her room Lily plugged in the charger on Bobby's phone and pressed the on switch. The phone bleeped, the screen lit up and Bobby's vibrant grin jumped out at her, making her gasp. It felt as if he was in there.

"Hello, Bob," she said. "Good job I know all your passwords."

The phone remained silent but his eyes seemed to look right at her, following her every move. It felt to Lily as if he wanted to show her something... Of course he did she realized, for he'd have Ali's details. She'd longed for ages to just pick up the phone and contact her but no one seemed to have her number...or if they did then they weren't saying.

Her fingers trembled as she clicked on *Ali* and the buzz of the ring tone echoed around inside her head.

"Hello...! Bobby!" Ali's voice, once so familiar, sounded shaky and odd.

"Ali... Ali," she cried. "It's me... Lily."

"Oh..." The phone went silent for a minute. "I thought... I mean... How are you all?"

"We're good... I guess. Sorry if I gave you a fright but Mum gave me the phone, you see... Bobby can't use it anymore after all and he wouldn't have minded."

"He'd have loved you to have his phone, Lily. I know it."

"Thanks... Mum says it's my Christmas present from him. Did you have a good Christmas? Ours was kind of quiet."

"I don't suppose you felt much like celebrating," Ali said. "I spent it with friends and their children...it was nice."

"I've wanted to talk to you for ages," Lily blurted out.

"But I didn't have your number and anyway everyone told me that I should leave well enough alone."

"And Tom?" Ali asked. "Did he say that, too?"

Lily shook her head. "He doesn't say much at all... I think he misses you though."

"You must have a good imagination if you think that, Lily... Anyway it looks like you just might have to put up with me again, for a while at least."

"What, you mean you're coming back...here...with your husband?"

For a moment Ali went quiet. "It's a long story, Lily," she said. "But I'll be on my own. I need to come back though, I realize it now. Anyway, I have to go but I'll speak to you soon I promise."

"But when...?" Lily began, and then the phone went dead.

WALKING ALONG THE bustling street, Ali felt lost in the sea of nameless faces that surrounded her. She'd once loved living in the city but now all she could think about was the peace and tranquility of Jenny Brown's Bay and her cottage on Cove Road. A heavy weight came over her and her feet seemed to drag as she headed back to the offices of *The Times*; she'd felt so tired lately but she guessed it must be all the trauma and emotion that seemed to color her life at the moment. She'd told Lily that she was going back to Jenny Brown's Bay and now it was time to act, not dream; tonight, she decided, she'd tell Jason and Laura that she was leaving.

COVE COTTAGES LOOKED just the same, thought Ali, as she pulled up outside Number Three, except that when she'd left in November it had all been so gray and wild. Now though the trees were rimed with a frost that sparkled in the crisp winter sunshine and the sky was a pale eggshell blue with a flurry of fluffy white clouds moving lazily across its wide expanse above a shimmering, peaceful sea.

Last night she'd slept at a travel lodge, needing space to clear her head. Jake rang twice but she didn't answer. She really had nothing left to say to him…except perhaps goodbye. By 7:00 a.m., after skipping breakfast, she'd been on the road again, heading for her whole new start. Now she suddenly realized, climbing out of her car, it was almost lunchtime and hunger pangs clawed.

As she looked out across the bay the clear, crisp air took her breath away; she gulped it deep down into her lungs as if to totally immerse herself in being back here in Jenny Brown's Bay. She'd take all her stuff inside, she decided, then light the fire to get the cottage warmed up and order in some supplies.

Carrying her bags and cases she headed for the front door of Number Three, her eyes drawn to Tom's cottage just down from her own. Was he home, she wondered, and would he be angry that she was back? The Roberts family had been grieving for months, learning to live with their loss; seeing her again might just churn up all the pain. Perhaps she was wrong to have come back here; perhaps she should have found another fishing village to go to, where she could do some more research and write her book without upsetting anyone. The book was about Bobby though, and this was Bobby's place; she had to be here. She'd just stay away from everyone as much as possible, go on the internet and get her supplies delivered from the store in town and absorb herself in her writing.

By late afternoon a fire was roaring up the chimney, she'd unpacked her suitcase ordered her supplies and dusted and cleaned up the cottage, opening all the windows to let in some fresh air, despite the cold. Then unable to resist the glorious view beyond her window she took a stroll along the shore, hoping she wouldn't see anyone. The walk made her feet and fingers tingle and when she got back to the cottage she knelt down in front of the fire holding her hands out to the flickering flames with a good feeling inside her.

She was sorry if her being here upset the Roberts brothers, but she needed this so much and she'd stay well away from them. Anyway, Tom's cottage was dark and empty so perhaps he'd moved out. That thought made her feel sad and lonely; she'd held a secret hope that maybe one day she and Tom could at least be friends again.

Her supplies arrived shortly after the winter's sun slid down into the bay, leaving the world outside the cottage in a silvery darkness. Opening the door to let the delivery man in with the boxes she noted that both the other two cottages in the row were still dark, so obviously Tom wasn't home yet. The owners of Number Two hadn't been around since she moved to Cove Road. Elsa May, her landlady, had said that they were working abroad and the cottage had been empty for over a year.

With a cheery smile the man deposited her supplies on the kitchen table. "Thanks," Ali said. He waved his hand, heading back towards his van.

It was just before she shut the door that she saw Tom walking home through the darkness.

He must have seen her in the light from the open door but he just stared straight ahead, striding out along the track toward his cottage as if he hadn't noticed she was there. So he was still angry with her. She fought back sadness. Never mind, she had plenty to fill her time now and she needed no one's company but her own.

FOR ALMOST THREE full days Ali spoke to no one. She walked along the shore in the early mornings wrapped up in her down-filled jacket, delighting in the smells and sounds of the sea as she watched Tom from afar, walking straight and resolute along the track that led to the village. Was he heading off to the boatyard or the pub? she wondered, wishing she could just go and ask him. And had he started fishing again or was Bobby's death still too raw? Maybe he'd fallen out of love with the sea since his brother's tragedy; somehow though she couldn't really believe that.

On the fourth day, as she leaned over her laptop immersed in her work, a knock came on her door. She sat up sharply, heart pounding, smoothing down her hair as she hurried to answer it. "Hello…"

"Hello," said Lily with a cautious smile. "Why didn't you tell me you were back?"

"BYE, MUM," TOM called. "I've fixed the bedroom door for you and the new kitchen unit's up so I'm off now."

Grace bustled ito the kitchen, eager to see her eldest son before he left. "Thanks, love," she said, kissing him on the cheek. "Now are you off to the boatyard or are you heading home?"

"Boatyard," Tom replied with no hesitation. "We might not be fishing today but there's always plenty to do."

"You need to live a little, Tom," she said. "Bobby's gone but that doesn't mean that you can't get on with your life."

Tom gave her shoulder a quick squeeze. "I am, Mum. I'm getting on with my life in my own way so don't worry about me."

"I worry about you all… It's what mothers do… Did you know that Ali has come back?"

He could hardly lie to his mother. "We both live on Cove Road...so yes, I had noticed."

"Have you spoken to her?"

Tom shrugged. "Why would I... I have nothing to say to her."

"She might need a friend...after all, according to Lily she went back to her husband and now she seems to be here all alone..."

The flicker of a smile softened Tom's features. "And how, Mother dear, have you managed to acquire all this information?"

"It's a small place," she told him, raising her eyebrows. "Bill, who delivers my groceries from the store in town, just happens to deliver to Ali, too. He was there the other day and he said that she seemed to be on her own."

Tom laughed. "And when did you become such a nosey parker?"

"I'm not a nosey parker," his mother said, affronted. "I just happen to care about people and no one wants to be alone...even if they think they do."

"I'm alone," responded Tom.

"And so is Bobby," came Ned's harsh voice from behind them. "Isn't that what's important? No one seems to care anymore."

They both looked at him in surprise. "Of course we care and of course it's important," Grace cried, her face crumpling. "He was my son, my baby boy. Somehow, Ned, we have to try and deal with it and remember the love and happiness we shared. He's gone and no amount of bitterness will bring him back."

When Ned strode off without replying Grace turned toward Tom, her face pale and sad. "Please talk to him, Tom, he won't talk to me and the only person he's going

to hurt by carrying around all that anger is himself…
Perhaps Ali could try and make him see sense."

"I think Ali is the last person to make Ned see sense,"
Tom said. "And it's obvious that she wants to be left
alone. Ned will come to accept Bobby's loss eventually…
It's just too soon for him yet that's all."

Tom thought about his brother as he worked on *The
Sea Hawk* later that day, getting her ready and shipshape
for their next trip. Perhaps it was Ned's own guilt, he decided, that made him so bitter; it wasn't like him to be
so negative, and to lay all the blame at Ali's door was
downright cruel. Sure, in a way it was her fault, but it
was Bobby who'd made all the fuss about bringing her
along and neither Ned, nor their dad for that matter, had
backed Tom up when he refused to take her. Anyway,
what was the point? It was all water under the bridge
now. Their mum had the right idea, she of all people
was the one most likely to feel bitter but all she said was
that they should just remember the love and happiness
they'd shared when Bobby was alive and rejoice in having known him.

Ned, though, was in a very dark place. Maybe his gut
instinct was right, Tom thought, and Ned did feel that
as an integral part of Search and Rescue he should have
been able to save their brother. Tomorrow, he decided,
putting his tools away, he'd try and talk to him again,
make him see sense.

Tom was just leaving the boatyard when his phone
blasted from his back pocket. He always had it set on a
rowdy tune; otherwise he'd never hear it. Now it jangled
in his ears annoyingly. swiping it open he put it to his
ear. "Hello…"

"Tom," came his mother's voice, high-pitched and anxious. "Have you seen Lily? It'll be dark soon and I don't know where she's got to."

"Don't worry, Mum," he told her. "You know Lily—no doubt she'll come sauntering in soon with her pockets full of pebbles and shells."

His mother's voice lightened and he knew he'd made her smile. "Actually she was looking for a carrier bag," she told him.

"There you go then," he said. "And don't worry—I'll soon track her down."

CHAPTER TEN

"WHY DIDN'T YOU tell me you were back?" asked Lily. Her lips curved into a smile but Ali could see the hurt in her eyes. Reaching out she took hold of the girl's slim pale hands and drew her into the cottage.

"I'm sorry," she said. "I wanted to tell you but I didn't want to cause any upset for anyone… I mean, I know how Ned feels but I'm not sure about Tom and your parents. Seeing me might bring all the pain back."

Lily shook her head. "The pain's still there but I think it's only Ned who really blames you. I mean, I know it was kind of your fault but Mum says it was just fate and you didn't mean it to happen… It was just one of those things."

"Of course I didn't mean it," Ali cried. "And I feel bad about what happened. Maybe I should talk to Ned."

Lily shrugged. "He won't listen. Here…"

She reached down and picked up a carrier bag from the floor. "I brought cake… I made it myself this morning. It's to say welcome."

Reaching out her arms Ali gave her a hug. "Oh Lily," she cried, her eyes filling with tears. "You really are the sweetest, nicest person I've ever met."

AS HE APPROACHED Cove Road Tom saw that Ali's front door was open, strengthening his hunch about Lily's whereabouts. The sun was slipping down over the horizon, turning the sea crimson and bringing a rosy glow to the windows of the cottages as he approached Number Three. He saw Lily at once, in the doorway; her back was toward him, and her fair hair cascaded over her shoulders, gleaming with rose from the sun. Ali was in front of her, her face glowing with such a glorious light that he felt his heart quicken.

Tom stood motionless as Ali drew his sister into her arms. What to do? Should he just walk away or should he walk boldly over and tell Lily that she was in trouble. She really had to stop these disappearing acts. What to say to Ali though?

He walked determinedly toward them, stopping tongue-tied in the doorway. "Lily," he eventually managed. "You know that you're supposed to tell Mum where you're going. She's worried about you."

Ali dropped her arms to her sides and Lily turned around to give her brother a sweet smile. "Sorry, Tom, I just forgot. I heard someone in the bar saying that Ali was back you see and I was so excited… I made her a cake. Perhaps you can come in and have some with us."

"Oh I don't think…" he began.

"He can…can't he, Ali?" Lily asked with her most appealing smile.

Ali glanced at Tom, holding his eyes for a moment. "Of course," she said. "If he wants to."

"He does," cried Lily. "Don't you, Tom?"

Tom shrugged. "I guess."

"I'll put the kettle on then," Ali said, heading into the kitchen.

It was strange, thought Tom, to be sitting in Ali's kitchen, watching her scurry about the room with quick determined movements. She looked nervous, he thought, and very strained.

Lily broke the awkwardness between them, asking outright the questions that were inside his head. "Why hasn't your husband come with you? Did you have a row or something?"

"Yes," Ali told her, pouring boiling water into the pot. "Some things just aren't meant to be."

"But you are going back to him…when he says sorry?"

Ali glanced sideways at Tom and looked away again. "No," she said slowly. "Sometimes sorry just isn't enough."

"My mum says you should always say sorry and then you can be forgiven."

Seeing a flash of pain in Ali's eyes, Tom cut in, "And doesn't Mum also tell you that you mustn't be too nosy?"

Lily just laughed. "Ali doesn't mind."

Ali giggled at that. "Oh Lily," she cried. "Never stop being so…just never stop being you."

"What…never stop being irritating, you mean?" Tom remarked with a smile.

"No," Ali objected. "Not irritating…more…refreshing, I guess."

Lily frowned, puzzled. "Ice lollies are refreshing."

"And so is a nice cool beer," Tom told her. "And you definitely aren't either of those. Anyway, I need to get you home so just eat your cake and we'll get off."

"Better still," suggested Ali. "Why don't I wrap it up for you and then you can take it home with you."

"Okay," Lily agreed. "But will you wrap Tom's, too?"

For a moment Ali seemed to hesitate. "He could always pick his up on the way back," she suggested without looking at him.

Lily nodded. "Okay…but can I come back and see you tomorrow?"

"Of course… You can come and see me any time you want, you know that. Just make sure you tell your mum where you are."

Tom walked beside his sister, listening with only half an ear to her chattering; the other half was firmly fixed on the gentle swishing of the waves as they lapped against the shore.

"So," she said. "*Do* you like her?"

He frowned. "Do I like who?"

"Ali of course… I'm sure she likes you."

"Oh Lil…" He stopped, giving her his full concentration. "You really must curb that wild imagination of yours you know. Ali is married. No doubt she'll make things up with her husband very soon, but even if she doesn't, I am certainly not looking for a relationship."

"You heard her," cried Lily. "She said they're over… and if it's Ned you're bothered about well I'm sure he'd soon get used to the idea."

Tom raised his eyebrows. "And do you really believe that?"

"Well it might take him a little time I guess…but I'm sure Mum and Dad wouldn't mind."

"Lily Roberts," Tom told her with an exasperated sigh. "You have to put any crazy ideas you may have about me and Ali out of your head right now. There are way too many complications for us to try to even be friends, let alone anything more…"

Tom thought about their conversation as he headed back toward Cove Cottages half an hour later. Could he and Ali ever get far enough past Bobby's tragedy to one day become friends? he wondered. An image of her face popped unbidden into his mind; the idea appealed to him. After all, they'd got on well enough once, he remembered, his mind going back to those early days when she stayed at the pub and they talked and talked about everything from fishing to life. Besides, bearing grudges wasn't in his nature. He increased his pace. But what would be the point? As he'd told Lily, she'd probably make it up with her husband soon and be off again. No, getting close to Ali would bring only regret. Keeping his distance was the wisest thing to do.

A warm yellow light shone from her front window and a sliver of smoke curled up from the chimney into the rapidly darkening sky. He'd just walk by, he decided; with a bit of luck she wouldn't see him.

But as he hurried past her door she called out to him. "Tom…! Don't forget your cake."

"Sorry," warmth flooded his face as he turned to face her. "I forgot all about it."

"No matter," she said, holding back the door. "Come on in, I'll get it for you."

Tom's eyes were irresistibly drawn to her as she removed the cake from its tin and lifted it carefully onto a plate. She moved so easily, like flowing liquid, and her shoulder-length blond-streaked hair shone with the warmth of honey, matching her eyes. Looking up she met his gaze with a smile. "Would you like to eat it here?" she asked. "I can brew a pot of tea…or maybe you fishermen prefer coffee."

"No…thanks." He sat down awkwardly on the chair she pulled out for him. The way he reacted to her felt wrong, awkward. Bobby's death was still too raw, and although he didn't really blame her, as Ned did, he felt a sense of guilt at being here with the woman his brother had been in love with. "I really need to get going," he said abruptly. "I can't stay long."

"I know, I'm sure you must have loads to do and I don't want to intrude. I just need to talk to you."

Tom stood, pushing back his chair. "I really don't have time," he began.

She placed her hand on his shoulder and he felt the

warmth of it through his jacket. "Please," she said. "It'll only take a minute."

"I'm not really much of a talker I'm afraid…"

"Then just listen," Ali suggested. "If I don't say this now then I may never get the chance again."

Tom frowned, feeling awkward. "Okay then," he said reluctantly, not wanting to get into anything heavy right now. "If you must…don't take too long though."

Ali took a deep breath then hesitated, and for a moment Tom thought she'd changed her mind. When she did start talking, to his surprise it was all about Bobby and how she met him at a charity do with her husband.

"Jake was his tutor," she said, with a tremble in her voice. "He was busy organizing things and Bobby and I sat and talked. He made me laugh so much that night but I never thought of him as anything other than just a boy, you know. He was a friend, that's all, when I needed one. A good friend who supported me in my grief over Dad's death. The fact that he was a fisherman brought us closer, too, I suppose—in fact he was the one who first gave me the idea of writing an article about fishing… for Dad. It was his kindness that prompted him to suggest that I stay at your parents' pub… Bobby was warm-hearted and good. He really cared about people and when he realized that things had gone wrong between me and Jake he wanted to help."

For a moment Ali went quiet, as if trying to collect her thoughts. Tom wanted to ask her what went wrong with her marriage but he kept his question to himself. She looked so sad and vulnerable that a part of him wanted to take her in his arms and tell her that everything was going to be okay…the other part wanted to walk away.

"When Bobby suggested that I come here it seemed like a godsend," she eventually went on. "Time to breathe and contemplate my life was just what I needed, and there was also the opportunity to research fishing and fishermen, for the article I wanted to write…"

"It wasn't a godsend for Bobby though was it," Tom blurted out, suddenly angry.

"Oh Tom," Ali cried, dropping her face into her hands. Her voice came out muffled from behind her fingers. "I am so, so sorry and I wouldn't blame you if you said you hated me. I should have listened when you warned me not to go on the fishing trip…and I should have stayed inside as you told me to and not been so foolish as to go out into the storm to spread my dad's ashes. It was all my fault and I've so wanted to apologize. Please don't hate me."

Reaching across the short distance between them he pressed his knuckles gently against her damp cheek. "I could never hate you," he said. "Accidents happen every day and what happened to Bob was a devastating tragedy. It can't be undone though and all we can do now is to try and find a way to live with what's happened and move on…and for what it's worth, I'm sorry your marriage didn't work out…he's a fool."

"No," Ali said, looking up with a ghost of a smile, "…not really a fool, just a double-crossing, two-timing loser."

"Well he's certainly a loser," Tom agreed.

"So do you mind if I stay around here for a while?"

"It's hardly up to me is it?"

To his surprise she took hold of his sleeve. "Walk along the beach with me a little way…please. I love to watch the moon rise over the bay and the sky's amazing tonight."

He wanted to say no…it wasn't wise…it was too soon. "Better get your coat," he suggested. "It may be beautiful but it's bitter out."

They walked in silence; hands plunged deep into their pockets for warmth as they took in the awesome scene in front of them. The sky, dark navy blue shot with silver and gray...and the sea, still a warm rosy hue from the evening sun that had just slipped out of sight. They paused in unison, drawn together by the magic that surrounded them, their bodies close but not quite touching.

She glanced up at him and her eyes seemed to melt into his, honey-warm and so, so, deep. "I'm sorry, Tom—" she murmured "—about everything."

His response was to hold out his arms, and when she stepped into them it felt so right...until the memories burst in; Bobby calling her name...giving his life to try and save hers.

"I have to go," he said, stepping abruptly away from her. "You need to sort out your life and decide what you want and I have to get my head straight."

"Can I talk to you at least?" Ali pleaded.

He hesitated. "About what?"

"Oh I don't know," she cried. "I feel like everything's such a mess and it's my fault...and then there's Jake."

"Your husband you mean?"

She nodded. "He cheated on me. Bobby never admitted it but I think he only suggested I come to Jenny Brown's Bay because he felt sorry for me—it seems all Jake's students knew that he and one of the other tutors were having an affair, everyone was talking about it. I felt such a fool."

"So why did you go back to him?" Tom asked.

Ali glanced up at him in surprise. "I didn't go back to him... I almost did, I admit that, because I still believe in the sanctity of marriage and the vows I took...in the end though I walked away." She looked at him, her eyes sparkling in the moonlight with unshed tears. "Perhaps that makes me a coward," she said quietly. "To walk away so easily from my responsibilities."

"Look…" On a sudden impulse Tom reached out to grip her forearm, still keeping a distance between them. "One thing I do know is that you are no coward. Look how you came to Bobby's funeral even though you thought that no one wanted you there."

"I almost didn't come," she admitted. "I almost just got into my car and drove away."

"But you didn't drive away and *almost* doesn't count."

"Thanks," she said simply.

"Just one more thing, Ali," Tom said as they started walking toward the cottages again, the warm lights glowing out into the soft darkness of the evening. "One thing I'd just like to clarify."

"Yes?" Ali sounded apprehensive.

"Did it ever occur to you that Bobby may have been in love with you?"

She stopped in her tracks. "Bobby! With me? But he was just a boy."

"He was a man, Ali, very much a man."

"That's why Ned hates me so much," she said as the truth began to dawn, then she stopped in her tracks, looking at Tom. "So do you hate me, too?"

The pale light of the moon revealed the uncertainty that flickered on her face. "I was angry with you," he admitted. "But I could never hate you. You were just naïve, I suppose, and maybe a little selfish."

"I was a fool," she cut in, holding Tom's gaze, almost daring him to question her admission. "A stupid, selfish fool who thought of nothing but her own problems… That's why Bobby jumped in to try and save me, isn't it, because of how he felt about me? That's why he died…"

An awareness of the painful truth burned between

them as he held her gaze. "It was an accident, Ali," he said quietly. "Caused by bizarre circumstances and maybe mistakes…but isn't that how all accidents occur?"

"We can never be friends, Tom, can we?" she asked, her voice breaking. "If you're right and your brother died for me, I should just walk away right now and never come back?"

"No!" His objection was instant, from the heart. "Only a coward would run away from this…like I said, it was a terrible accident and we need time, time to heal and accept what's happened. Just be honest with yourself, Ali. Be honest with everyone and one day…one day who knows what might happen."

Reaching out she took hold of his hands. "What do you mean, Tom?" she asked hopefully. "What might happen?"

He shrugged, allowing his fingers to rest in hers. "Only time will tell us that."

"Oh Tom, I'm so, so sorry," she said, releasing her hold.

He allowed his hands to fall back against his sides, clenching his fingers into fists. "It was an accident," he repeated. "A collection of circumstances that went tragically wrong, but it's done now. Bobby's gone and we all have to live with that, perhaps you more than anyone."

He watched her as she headed back toward her cottage without another word, a huge weight of regret in his heart.

CHAPTER ELEVEN

ALI THRASHED AND turned in her bed unable to sleep, plagued by what was now so obvious to her. She'd been such a selfish fool. What must Tom really think of her, what must everyone think of her? That she'd led poor Bobby on for her own ends. In her mind it hadn't been like that. She hadn't realized how he felt about her; at least Tom had seemed to believe her when she'd told him she really didn't know, but still it made her seem totally self-absorbed. So absorbed by her own problems that she hadn't given anyone else's a thought.

Small unnoticed incidents came into her mind. Bobby grabbing her hand with an impish smile and holding it tight as they walked together, swinging it back and forth; Bobby, giving her a hug when she was down…and paying her teasing compliments that made her laugh. It all suddenly made sense.

As her eyes finally started to droop she felt Tom's arms again, holding her close, keeping her safe; a sob rose inside her…if only things had been different. But things weren't different, were they, she thought as her eyes burst back open and reality rushed in, and why should Tom Roberts want to keep *her* safe? Feeling sorry for herself wasn't going to help anyone, she had to be strong and put others first, starting with the book that Jason had suggested she write, a book to celebrate Bobby's life… a fisherman's life.

Running down the narrow stairs in her dressing gown she sat at the kitchen table and opened her laptop. The clock on the wall struck 2:00 a.m. but she ignored it as she read through the notes she'd done. Bobby's voice was everywhere, cracking jokes, singing in the pub, working on *The Sea Hawk* with Tom. He'd taught her how to bait hooks, what the best bait was to catch each type of fish, which equipment was required and how you should look after it. She'd typed out all the information in note form to sort out later.

And Tom was in there, too, telling her about his craft with a passion he couldn't withhold, so much material and so much emotion that it really could fill a book. And that, she decided, was what it would be…not the article she'd first intended but a book and she'd call it… She closed her eyes, concentrating; *A Fisherboy's Tale*, that's it. It would be fiction, but based on fact, an adventure story that would inspire a passion for the sea and a love of fishing in any young lad, and it would be dedicated to Bobby Roberts. She couldn't wait to start.

By six thirty Ali had finished the first chapter. Stretching her arms above her head she yawned, switching off her computer. It was time to get some sleep; and as she snuggled up beneath her duvet, closing her eyes against the world as dawn filtered in through her window, she felt a kind of peace slip over her; she was finally doing something positive, something she could lose herself in to forget all the heartache.

Tom was very much awake and ready for the fishing trip he, Ned and their dad had planned. He pulled his jacket more closely around his shoulders against the winter's chill as he headed out into the pale early morning light, glancing up at the noisy, hungry gulls that were already circling in the sky above. As he passed by Ali's cottage he slowed his steps, thinking about their conversation the night before and wishing things were different. In another time and another place he and Ali could have... what...been friends, or was it more than that?

He was attracted to her, he couldn't deny that, and he also felt protective of her. Despite what had happened, or perhaps because of it, she seemed vulnerable and very alone and he was sure she'd told him the truth about her feelings for Bobby. Ned was wrong about them. Last night she'd seemed so open and honest. Obviously she was the kind of person who acted on impulse but perhaps that was one of the very things about her that appealed to him. He thought everything through so carefully that her spontaneity was like a breath of fresh air.

He looked determinedly ahead. Whatever it was about her that drew him, he had to get past it. There was too much heartache and history between them now, too much blame and regret for them ever to be more than casual friends, and at the moment they weren't really even that.

Sometimes he wished he was more like his sister, Lily; for her life was not so complicated. She took people at face value, listened to what they said and interpreted it in her own openhearted way. Their mother always said that because nature had let Lily down in some departments it had given her other, special, senses to compensate; Lily believed wholeheartedly in Ali and she'd already told him that she was going to make it her personal challenge to help them get together. As usual, thinking of his sister brought a smile to Tom's face.

"THERE'S FOUR NOW, MUM," Lily called through to the kitchen. "And all the pups seem really healthy."

Grace Roberts appeared in the doorway; her round face flushed from the stove. "Don't you think you'd better ring Tom?" she said. "After all, Pip is really his dog."

Hearing her name the little white terrier with one brown patch over her eye wriggled her whole body while still eagerly licking her pups.

"Look how pleased she is with herself," Lily cried with delight. "And Tom's gone out fishing so I'll wait until he comes back to tell him he's a grandad."

Grace threw her hands in the air with a burst of the ready laughter that had been so rare of late. "Does that mean I'm a great-grandma then?"

"I guess so," Lily said, smiling. "And, Mum…"

"Yes?"

"It's good to hear you laughing again."

AFTER A SUCCESSFUL day's fishing Tom was just about to head homeward when his phone jangled in his pocket. "Hi, Lily," he said. "What's up?"

"It's Pip," cried his sister, her voice high-pitched with excitement. "She's had four pups. You have to come and see them."

"Wow, I didn't think she was due for a couple of days yet. Thanks for looking after her Lil, I'll be round shortly…and she's okay?"

"She's a great mum and she's so proud of herself."

Tom strode eagerly toward the village and The Fisherman's Inn. Pip might technically be his dog, but after he moved into his cottage she'd kept going back to the pub, so he'd let Lily look after her there, and although Pip was always excited to see him there was no doubt about where she thought she belonged. She loved to wander around the bar, searching for scraps and charming the patrons. At first her defection had hurt, but he'd come to realize that his cottage was way too quiet for her and she just loved being in the pub.

As soon as he walked in through the door of the back kitchen where her whelping box was, Pip wagged her tail when she saw him, proudly nudging her puppies. "You clever girl," he told her, crouching down to scratch the backs of her ears.

"Aren't they just gorgeous," sighed Lily, "Especially the one with the freckles and a brown patch over its eye."

"Well I can't believe she got in pup in the first place," Tom said. "I should have had her spayed already but I thought there were no dogs around here and we never let her out on her own anyway. She's definitely going to get done now, that's for sure."

Lily giggled. "I think I know who the dad is."

"*Now* you tell me…bit late isn't it?"

"I didn't know at the time," Lily assured him. "I just thought about it and remembered that couple who stayed here with their West Highland terrier. I didn't think they ever let it off the lead but the dates tie up."

"You minx, Pip," Tom said. The little dog looked up at him, her eyes shining with pride, and he laughed. "Well at least your suitor was a pedigree."

Lily clasped her hands together, looking up at him appealingly. "Please, please, please can I have one, Tom?"

"Of course…first pick."

"And… I've had an idea…"

"Yes?"

"You could give one to Ali, you know, to show her that you're a friend. I don't think she has that many and having a dog to keep her company would stop her being lonely."

Tom hesitated. "I'm not sure about that, Lil," he said slowly. "And how do you know that she's lonely anyway?"

Lily shrugged. "I can just tell... Please Tom. It would be a really nice thing to do."

"I'll think about it," he promised, "but what about the other two?"

"Well I thought you might want to keep one for yourself and we can easily find a good home for the other, they're so cute."

Tom frowned. "I don't know about that. I'll think about it. There's plenty of time to decide."

"Only eight weeks," Lily reminded him. "So you'll have to hurry up."

HUNGER PANGS WOKE Ali midafternoon. She rolled over, bleary-eyed, trying to get her bearings and bolting upright as reality hit. It was the same every time she woke; her sense of security and peace would suddenly dissolve to reveal all the agony of the last few months. At least now she had a purpose to get up.

She went into the kitchen to make herself a sandwich and a cup of coffee. Just as she was pouring the boiling water into the pot, a voice sounded right behind her. Ali jumped, almost spilling the scalding water.

"Lily!" she cried. "For heaven's sake, I could have easily burned us both and I'm in enough trouble with your family as it is. Think how mad they'd be if I'd ended up taking you to A&E with second-degree burns."

Lily's pale face turned pink. "Sorry... I did shout hello...and anyway, you aren't in trouble with my family...at least not with Tom."

"Did he tell you that?"

"Well...no." Lily squirmed, two bright spots appearing on her cheeks. "But..."

Ali put down the kettle and took both her hands. "I'm

sorry, Lily," she said. "You took me by surprise that's all. Would you like a cookie?"

Easily placated, Lily grinned. "Yes please... Pip's had her pups by the way. Tom says I can have one for my own. You'll have to come and see them."

"Oh I don't know about that... I don't think I'd be very welcome at the pub."

"Mum wouldn't mind and you could come when Ned's at work."

"Why don't you just take some pictures for me?" Ali suggested.

Lily nodded eagerly. "That's a brilliant idea—I could take them on my phone." She hesitated. "Do you like dogs?"

Ali handed her the cookie jar with a smile. "Yes, of course, I had a dog of my own when I was a girl."

Lily carefully chose a cookie and extracted it with her thumb and forefinger. "What happened to it?"

"It got old and died," Ali said with a sigh. "It happens to all God's creatures eventually but it always makes us sad."

"Was Bobby one of God's creatures?" Lily asked.

Ali looked at her in surprise. "Why...yes," she said. "Of course he was... We are all God's creatures."

"Would you like another dog?"

Thrown as usual by Lily's direct line of questioning, Ali shrugged. "One day perhaps, when I'm settled."

"But aren't you settled now?"

"Do you know," Ali admitted. "I'm not really sure. I mean, I love it here but I'm only renting this cottage and so much has happened. I don't really think I'm very welcome here and that makes me feel awkward... If I tell you a secret will you keep it to yourself?"

Lily touched her finger to her lips. "I'm a good secret-keeper... I've got lots of secrets."

"Like what?"

"If I told you they wouldn't be secrets... Anyway, what's yours? I promise not to tell even if it's bad."

"It's not at all bad," Ali said. "In fact it's good I hope... I'm writing a book."

Lily frowned. "I already knew that...didn't I?"

"Well yes but this is...this is a proper book, you know, a novel. It's set in Jenny Brown's Bay and it's about some boys growing up, having adventures while they learn to be fishermen."

"What, you mean like Tom and Ned and Bobby?"

"Well they won't be called those names, but yes, it will be based on them... It's for Bobby you see."

Lily clasped her hands together in excitement. "That's brilliant. Can I tell Tom...please...? He'll be so happy."

"Tell me what?" Tom's voice floated through from the hallway, taking them both by surprise. "Sorry," he added. "The door was open and I heard Lily's voice. What is it you want to tell me, Lily?"

"It's a secret," Lily announced. "So I can't tell you."

"You've been warned about keeping secrets, Lil," he said, frowning.

"Sorry," Ali cut in. "It's my fault—I shouldn't have asked her to."

"No you shouldn't," Tom said abruptly. "It's not healthy... Anyway, come on, Lil, you're supposed to be working. You know Mum needs your help. She has no idea of time, that's the trouble," he added, for Ali's benefit.

As Lily ran off outside Ali looked boldly up at Tom, holding his gaze. "I'm sorry about the secret," she said. "It was nothing to worry about, honestly... Anyway, I didn't expect to be seeing you so soon again…after last night."

He frowned. "And you wouldn't have if I hadn't come looking for Lily…again. We've always instilled in her not to keep secrets. It could be dangerous, you see…for a girl as naïve as Lily."

"Honestly, it wasn't like that," Ali insisted. "I think the world of her and I would never be irresponsible where she's concerned."

For just a moment his expression softened. "I'm sure you wouldn't, I just overreact sometimes… Anyway…" Suddenly he smiled. "What is your secret?"

"You'll know soon enough," she promised. "Anyway… see you around…again."

"See you around," he echoed, his dark eyes lingering for just a moment.

"Come on, Tom," yelled Lily from outside and with a brief lift of his hand he was gone.

CHAPTER TWELVE

FOR THE NEXT FEW WEEKS Ali worked diligently on her book, alone apart from when Lily breezed in and made her smile, but happy in her own company. She tried not to think about Tom because her feelings for him were confusing and she needed to focus.

As the story progressed, taking shape in her mind, she began to feel as if she really knew Bobby, the real Bobby not just the bright, fun-loving young man who'd done his best to impress her. And she could see now that he had. Tom was right, Bobby really had been fond of her, maybe even imagined he was in love with her. But no matter what Ned and Tom thought it had only ever been just a boyhood crush…hadn't it?

The horror of that awful day flooded her mind. Bobby's voice desperately calling out to her as she hung above the water. She'd tried so hard to hold on to him when he fell but the awesome might of the cruel sea had torn him away. She'd always loved the sea in all its guises…now she wanted to hate it.

She walked across to the window, looking out across the serenity of the bay with a new respect, knowing that no matter what, she could never really hate the sea. Today it looked so tranquil and so very, very, beautiful that it seemed impossible for it to have taken Bobby's life…if she was honest, though she knew that she was the one who'd caused his death. The sea wasn't to blame…it was her irresponsibility and ignorance…

Her relationship with Bobby had been irresponsible, she knew that now. Ned was right, she may not have been having a love affair with Bobby but she had used him to make herself feel better about Jake's cheating and taken the kindness he offered without considering *his* feelings.

He'd bolstered her own lack of self-esteem by giving her the attention she craved and she should have realized how he felt and backed off…for his sake. So Ned was right and she *was* to blame for Bobby's death. After all, would he have jumped into the sea for someone he saw as just a friend? She pushed back her chair, leaped up and grabbed her coat, needing to get away from the dark thoughts that stifled her.

Tom REACHED DOWN to give Pip's ears a scratch, watching as she jumped back into the whelping box and cuddled with her pups, nudging them toward her teats as if she'd done it all a dozen times before.

"How does she know what to do?" Lily asked, her pretty face puckered in concentration. "If I had a baby I wouldn't know what to do and I can talk. Pip can't ask anyone she just has to do it all by herself…so how does she know?"

Tom shrugged. "I guess it's nature. How do swallows know to fly to Africa and back, or cod know when and where to move in the ocean?"

"Or trees know when to shed their leaves," Lily added.

"Or daffodil bulbs know when it's time to start growing into flowers…"

Tom looked across at his sister with affection. "We humans have to ask each other about such things, but nature just does them by instinct you see…and that's amazing."

"So do you think that if we humans couldn't speak to each other then we'd automatically know what to do?"

"I would hope so ," Tom told her. "So you don't need to worry about it."

"Have you asked Ali yet?" Lily's sudden change of subject took Tom by surprise. He should be used to her sudden swings in conversation by now.

"No," he announced. "And I don't want you to either… or at least not yet. I'm still thinking about it."

TWENTY MINUTES LATER, having called in to see his parents, Tom headed along the seafront toward Cove Road. He saw Ali coming out of Number Three as he walked down the narrow pathway toward the cottages but it was obvious that she hadn't noticed him. Her jacket was unbuttoned despite the cold and her hair blew out behind her in a cloud, dancing on the blustery wind. She looked upset, he thought, following in her footsteps.

When she stopped down by the sea, where a clump of gray rocks rose up from the rushing tide, he stopped, too. He didn't want to interfere but…

She sat down on the rocks, staring out at the incoming sea, looking like a stranded mermaid. Then she looked down at her hands, twisted her wedding ring round on her finger and pulled it off, throwing it into the waves. He headed toward her, moving quietly across the sand. "You okay?" he asked, stepping up beside her. She was crying he noticed with a flood of dismay.

"Not really," she said.

"Want to talk about it?"

"Not really," she repeated.

"Let's walk," he suggested, waiting patiently while she got to her feet.

They headed along the shore with the sharp wind in

their faces, turning their cheeks to ice and making their eyes water. Ali shuddered, pulling her jacket more tightly around her. "I'm sorry," she said. "I was just having a wobbly moment…you need to go home now. I'll be fine."

"You threw away your ring…so is this all about your husband?"

Her response was emphatic. "No…that's all behind me now."

"Bobby then?"

When she nodded, dropping her chin to her chest, he stopped and took hold of her shoulders, turning her to face him. The pale winter's sun, slowly sinking toward the horizon, lit up her delicate features. Her honey-brown eyes, shadowed now, looked up into his.

"Look," he said. "We all have bad moments when it really gets to us, probably always will, but it's done now. We just have to learn to live with it."

"But it was my fault… I realize that now more than ever."

"What do you mean…what's changed?"

"You were right," she told him. "You know…about Bobby having feelings for me. I see it now and I feel so bad. I was just too busy thinking about my own problems to notice."

"So what's brought all this on now?" he asked.

"I've been thinking that's all, about Bobby and what happened. I didn't know…should have known. I was so selfish."

"There's something different," he said. "Something you're not telling me."

For a moment she hesitated. "Yes," she said. "There is something. The secret I asked Lily to keep…you need to know about it."

They walked back toward Number Three without

speaking. Tom's emotions spiraled out of control. One moment he wanted to walk away and the next he wanted to just take her in his arms and comfort her. What was the secret she was keeping, and why was she telling him this now?

THE FRONT DOOR creaked loudly as Ali pushed it shut behind them. The howling wind died away as it closed with a thud, leaving a heavy, lingering silence that made them both feel awkward.

"In here," she said, motioning him into the kitchen. Her voice sounded too loud in her ears. His presence beside her loomed too huge.

She picked up her notes, flicking on the laptop. The title of the book jumped out at her: *A Fisherboy's Tale*.

Tom frowned, his eyes racing over the page. "What's this?"

"This is the secret I told you about."

"Your article you mean?"

"It's a book…for Bobby."

"A book," he repeated. "What, you mean a story, like fiction?"

"It's a novel, but based on facts," she told him, her conviction fading as she saw the doubt in his eyes. "I've been writing notes since I got here, you already know that. A lot of the information came from the times I used to pick your brain in the pub."

He frowned. "But wasn't that all about the article for your dad?"

"It was, yes, but then I got to thinking that it would be nice to do something for Bobby. I'll write the article for my dad later. Anyway, while I was going through everything I got the idea to bring Bobby's early years back to life…and yours, if you don't mind. Basically it's about a young boy growing up in a fishing village with his two older brothers, learning to be fishermen. Bobby is the main character of course, but obviously I don't call him Bobby. The plot is based on the adventures they have while learning their trade. Obviously that's all fictitious, but I'll base it on the stories you told me. That way it'll be really authentic and hopefully Bobby's character will be authentic, too…if you'll help me. I want the book to be a real tribute to Bobby, a celebration of his life and a way of remembering him with joy instead of sorrow."

When Tom still didn't speak Ali's heart started racing. "But what about the things you said earlier, about it all being your fault?" he asked. "What does this story have to do with that?"

Her head fell to her chest. "The notes I made, they were about the people, too, not just the details about fishing as a way of life. When I read them Bobby came alive again, his humor, his kindness, his love for his family… his feelings for me. I felt that I was uncovering a whole new side of him that I hadn't appreciated before…and that's when I realized…"

"Realized what?"

"Realized that I needed to write this story…and—" she looked up at him, her eyes wide with tears "—and that Bobby hoped for more from me than just the friendship I so appreciated. I thought of him as just a boy, you see, but it suddenly struck me that maybe he was a little in love with me."

"More than a little," Tom agreed, his voice gruff with contained emotion.

"If you knew, then why didn't I?" she cried. "If I'd let him know where we stood right from the start then maybe he wouldn't have thrown his life away so easily. I should have seen it."

"But you didn't," Tom reminded her. "And tearing yourself up about it isn't going to bring him back."

"I need to think," she said. "You know, to get my head straight about it."

He stepped toward her, and when she looked up at him, he cupped her face between his hands and touched his lips to hers with a soft, sweet gentleness that brought a quiver to her whole body.

"Finish your book," he said, drawing back. "It's a good idea. I'll help you if I can…and so will Lily I'm sure."

"But," she began, touching her fingers to her lips.

"I'm not apologizing for the kiss," he told her with the flicker of a smile. "And I don't regret it, but now isn't about us, it's about what happened to Bobby, and us all getting past the guilt and regret before we can move on with our lives."

"Do you think Ned will ever get past it?"

Tom shrugged. "I hope so, eventually. Maybe your book will be the key. Perhaps when he reads it he'll see things differently."

"I hope so," Ali said. "And Tom?"

"Yes?"

"Thanks."

As she watched him walk away, two doors down to his lonely cottage, she felt a shudder of regret. Had she missed out on the love of her life? If the timing had been right could things have been different between her and Tom Roberts? She would probably never know, and now there was so much bitterness, heartache and regret to get past before she could even think about what *she* wanted. And anyway, did she even deserve to have the love of her life? She'd failed with Jake and she'd let Bobby and his family down so badly; her job now was just to try and make amends.

... "I'm really sorry," she said, her eyes searching his face anxiously.

"It's fine," he answered dully. "I guess I'm just trying to make sense of this. I don't understand how this happened."

CHAPTER THIRTEEN

As Ali walked down into the village a fluttering panic made the breath catch in her throat. Since her "moment" with Tom she'd kept herself to herself, writing constantly and seeing no one, except for Lily, who wouldn't stay away. Now, when Lily had finally managed to persuade her to go out, she was struggling to stay calm.

"What's up?" Lily asked, seeing Ali glancing around self-consciously. Her big blue eyes were round with curiosity as she skipped down the road, dressed in pale blue skinny jeans and a thick down navy jacket.

"Nothing," Ali insisted. "I just haven't been out in a while that's all... And I definitely should have worn a warmer jacket."

Lily pushed her hands deep into her pockets, hunching her shoulders. "Like mine?" she said, raising her eyebrows.

"Yes, like yours...plus..." Ali held her discerning gaze for a moment. Lily might be naïve in some ways, but she also had an awareness that could be quite disconcerting.

"Plus what?" Lily asked.

"Oh I don't know." Ali increased her pace. "I guess I worry that people are talking that's all."

"Talking about what?"

Ali forced what she hoped was a carefree smile onto her face. Truth was, after her realization about the way Bobby had felt about her, she had been shaken by guilt and suddenly everyone she met seemed to be looking at her with accusation in their eyes. "Nothing... I'm just being silly," she said. "I need to get out more."

"No one blames you, you know," Lily told her in a matter-of-fact tone. "It wasn't your fault that Bobby was in love with you."

"But I should have recognized that before it was too late," Ali admitted.

Lily stopped, taking both Ali's hands in hers. "My mum says that you can't change fate. It doesn't matter how anyone felt about anyone, what happened would still have happened. Now look, here comes, oh what's her name? You know...from the vet's. She's a receptionist there and you sometimes used to talk to her in the pub. Just try saying hello to her and then watch her eyes to see if there's any blame in them."

"It's Annie," Ali hissed, feeling like this was a test of sorts as the woman's small, brightly dressed figure drew closer.

"Hi, you two," Annie called. "I didn't realize that you were back, Ali. Are you here to stay now?"

Ali shrugged. "I'm not sure yet...although I do love Jenny Brown's Bay."

"Then stay," Annie told her. "It's not too far to commute to the city either, if you still want to keep your job as a journalist I mean."

"See," Lily whispered in her ear, making Ali smile. "No blame." She turned toward Annie , her blue eyes totally innocent of guile. "You don't blame Ali for Bobby's accident do you?"

Annie shuffled awkwardly from foot to foot. "Why... no," she said, taken aback. "Of course not."

"You see," Lily said with a happy smile, looking at Ali. "Annie doesn't blame you and neither will anyone else."

"Sorry," Ali apologized. "Lily does have a very direct way with her."

Annie nodded. "That's okay… I've been the brunt of Lily's questions before…and for what it's worth I don't think anyone really blames you…"

"Except Ned," cut in Lily.

Annie's cheeks turned a bright shade of rose. "Well… yes, but he's just hitting out I guess. Grief often wants to lay blame."

On impulse Ali reached out and placed her hand on the sleeve of the woman's red wool jacket. "Thank you," she said. "I can see that you understand the situation and I appreciate your honesty."

"Everyone around here understands," Annie told her. "You're in the country now you know and your business is everyone's business I'm afraid."

AFTER TALKING TO ANNIE, Ali felt much more confident; she purchased the items she needed from the village shop without even wondering if the shopkeeper was judging her and, on a sudden impulse she also bought a large chocolate bar. She handed it to Lily with a warm smile when they reached The Fisherman's Inn. "Thank you," she said, kissing her quickly on the cheek.

"But I haven't done anything," Lily said, puzzled.

"You've given me some self-confidence back," Ali told her. "And that's worth way more than just a chocolate bar."

"Come and see the puppies," Lily pleaded. "They're in the old back kitchen so you won't have to go into the pub, or even into Mum's big kitchen."

Ali hung back, wondering if Ned was around. "Oh I don't know," she said cautiously.

Lily's forehead puckered in disappointment. "But I thought you'd got your self-confidence back," she said.

"And I have," Ali declared, suddenly decided. "Lead on then, Lil."

WALKING BACK TO Cove Road half an hour later, Ali felt much happier than she had in weeks. Seeing the tiny squirming puppies with their ecstatic mum had really made her smile, making her realize that life went on no matter what. The smallest of the brood, white, cute and covered in freckles with a brown patch over one eye, just like Pip's, had really pulled at her heartstrings. In fact, if she'd been more permanently settled she'd have loved nothing better than to give it a home; it would be so nice to have a creature to care for, a little friend to keep her company.

The timing was all wrong though, she knew that. Her goal now was to keep a low profile and finish her book, for Bobby. There was nothing else she could think of to try and show just how much she cared, and if Ned did decide to have another go at her then she'd remember what Mary said about grief needing to strike out and lay blame.

As the days rolled by her life settled into a routine of endless writing. She saw hardly anyone except Lily and occasionally Tom. On the days when he dropped by, always unexpectedly, she would ask him all the questions she had stored up in her head, about Bobby and his childhood and what it was like to grow up with fishing in your blood.

It was strange the way they were together, never awkward but just professional and businesslike, like two work colleagues with a common purpose. For Ali it felt as if their "moment" had never been and she knew that was for the best, but sometimes, when she lay in her bed at night, all alone and struggling to sleep, if-only's would fill her head, flooding her veins with regret.

Apart from Tom's occasional visits, Ali's main link with humanity and life was through Lily, who turned up most days with a bright smile on her face, retelling amusing conversations she'd overheard in the pub and relaying snippets of gossip. She liked to talk about Tom, too, and her clumsy attempts at matchmaking made Ali smile, even though she knew it was too late for them.

For once though Lily hadn't called in and Ali had spent the whole Friday alone. As the long day drew to a close she stared blankly at her computer screen, blinking away the fatigue in her eyes as her thoughts turned to Tom. Anticipation fluttered as she remembered that Friday was one of the days he sometimes stopped by on his way home from work. Would he call in today? Did she want him to? A pulse beat in her throat as she remembered their "moment." She usually tried not to think about it but somehow today she couldn't get it out of her mind. OUTSIDE HER WINDOW she could see the sun sinking toward the horizon. A cluster of fluffy white clouds, rimmed with red, drifted across the blue-gray sky, and the incoming sea shimmered as it rippled up the sand. Closing her laptop she blinked, rubbing her eyes as she stood up. Her phone jangled harshly in the silence and when Jake's name jumped out at her she almost dismissed the call; he was the last person she needed to talk to. With a sigh she pressed the accept button. "Jake, I really haven't got anything to say to you," she began.

For a moment there was silence on the line. "What do you mean?" he eventually asked.

"I told you, Jake, we're over. I want a divorce and I've already spoken to a lawyer."

"What, so this really is it. I thought you just needed a bit of time to cool down."

Ali took a breath, realizing with astonishment that she felt totally detached from him, as if all the turmoil he'd put her through had never even happened. She liked the feeling. "Actually, Jake, I had no cooling down to do," she said. "I'm not even angry with you anymore and I really do have nothing to say to you."

When the line went dead she just sat for a moment, listening to the silence with a sense of triumph. She was over him, totally and finally without any lingering anger. It felt like a new beginning. And perhaps when she'd finished her book and finally put Bobby to rest she'd find there was a way forward for her. Perhaps she'd finally be able to let the past go and get on with living her life.

CHAPTER FOURTEEN

TOM AND NED worked in silence on *The Sea Hawk*, preparing her for the following week's fishing trip. Dressed in thick quilted jackets and gloves to keep out the cold, they struggled to sort through their fishing gear; when Ned cursed with frustration it occurred to Tom just how much things between them had changed over the last weeks. They used to laugh and joke together when they were working, despite the cold, but for ages now there'd been a barrier between them when they'd once been so close; it hurt, if he was honest, and it was about time he tried to do something about it.

"What is it with you, Ned?" he asked in a determinedly casual tone. "Ever since…ever since the accident you've had some kind of chip on your shoulder, but don't you think it's about time you got over it? Nothing will bring Bobby back and we have to get on with our lives you know."

"Well you certainly are," Ned snapped.

Tom fought back a rush of anger. "If this is still about Ali then it's time you let it go. She has her demons to deal with, too."

"She deserves everything she gets… It's you who's the fool but you just can't see it."

Ignoring Ned's remark Tom put away his tools and picked up his bag. "I'm off home," he said but his brother stepped in front of him, blocking his way.

"So is that it?" he exclaimed. "Aren't you even going to give me an argument?"

"Don't you think that we've already suffered way too much," Tom said, shaking his head sadly, "Why would I want to fight with you? Okay, I can see that you're still bitter about Ali and you're entitled to your opinion. I don't agree with you but that's as far as it goes."

"You have to admit that there must have been something going on between her and Bobby," Ned went on, refusing to drop the subject. "Let's face it, Tom, it was her fault that our brother died so how can you even speak to her…and I know you do?"

"Lily speaks to Ali all the time and you never say anything to her."

"Lily's a law unto herself. She doesn't think like we do."

"What, you mean she takes people for who they are with no prejudgment?"

A flush of color ran up Ned's neck, disappearing into his thick dark beard. "Look," he said. "I'm sorry, Tom, but I just can't seem to get past it… I mean, do you trust her…honestly?"

"Yes," Tom said. "I do."

"What, without even a glimmer of doubt?"

"No… I mean… Yes."

"You see," cried Ned in triumph. "You do have doubts."

"You're talking rubbish," Tom told him. "I'm off home."

As he headed for Cove Road, Tom went over and over their conversation. Ali had told him the truth the day he'd confronted her, he was sure of it…wasn't he? The answer came instantly; of course he did… Yet still he walked slowly, his head going round in circles. It was Ned who was putting doubts in his mind again...

As he dropped down into the cove where the row of terraced cottages sat right by the shore, he stopped to stare at the scene that never failed to lift his spirits. Way up ahead of him the evening sun was setting, outlining the purple-gray clouds with crimson edges and turning the sea that stirred the sand into a shimmering frothy mass of molten gold. The windows of Ali's cottage glinted gold, too, he noticed, seeming to wink at him, and he found himself walking toward her front door. He had intended to give calling in on her a miss tonight after Ned had messed with his head but he needed to see her, needed to know that his gut feeling about her was true and she'd been totally honest with him about Bobby.

TOM KNOCKED ON the door of Number Three and then knocked harder. He tried the door and when it opened to his touch he walked into the hallway, calling her name. Ali was often too engrossed in her writing to hear his knock and he'd gotten into the habit of just walking in when he stopped in on his way home, or when he was looking for Lily.

Today she was sitting at the kitchen table as usual, but her laptop was closed in front of her and she looked different, numb and distracted. "What's up," he asked.

She glanced at him her eyes wide with surprise. "It's just hit me that I'm getting divorced I guess," she said. "Jake, my husband, rang and I felt nothing for him. It all seems like such a waste."

"But if you really are over him with no regrets then isn't that a good thing. Perhaps you should be celebrating."

She shook her head determinedly. "No...not yet anyway, maybe when the divorce is final and my book's finished."

"How long were you married?" As the words left his lips Tom immediately wished that he could retract them. He never asked Ali personal questions when he called in. Mostly they just talked about Bobby and their childhood in Jenny Brown's Bay for her book. In a way, the closeness that had grown between them because of Bobby now seemed to have pushed them further apart, making him feel as if anything more personal between them would be a blot on his brother's memory.

Today though, hearing Ali talk about her husband and divorce changed things; this wasn't all about Bobby anymore, it was about two people dealing with the crises life had flung at them. A woman whose marriage had gone wrong and whose friendship had ended in tragedy, and a man—for a moment Tom thought about himself, trying to be honest—a man who was struggling to come to terms with so many demons and shifting emotions that included his feelings for a woman who was wrong for him. Talking to her about Bobby had brought back his brother's bright, caring, fun personality, bringing him and Ali very close. Deep down he wished that closeness was more than just friendship; he wanted to hold her, to make her a part of his life. Those feelings were buried though, deep down inside and that was where they had to stay.

"Two years," she said. "We were married for two years."

"And it really is over?" He couldn't help the lightening of his voice as he asked her the question.

"Yes," she said. "It really is over… How can you believe that you love someone and make promises and vows that are supposed to last forever when it all turns out to have been a sham?"

Tom shrugged, feeling helpless. "I don't know."

"So how do you ever know that what you feel for someone really is love…? How can you know if it's going to last?"

Seeing the intensity in her face Tom recognized with a sudden jolt just how strong his feelings for her were; and that was why he had to keep his distance. "I guess you just follow your gut," he said.

She nodded slowly, looking up at him. "I suppose I followed my gut instinct coming back here."

"I'm glad you did," he said without thinking. "I mean, I think it was the right thing for you to do."

"Even though all your family's heartache was caused by me?"

"It's down to fate, not you," he told her. "And at least you're trying to help by writing the book."

"Thanks," she said. "It means a lot…and thanks for your input."

Tom placed his hand on her shoulder; the warmth of her skin beneath his palm, through the thin stuff of her shirt, made his heart rate quicken. "I'm just glad I could help," he said. "And for what it's worth I think the book is a great idea."

Ali reached up her hand to cover his fingers momentarily with hers. "Getting to know Bobby so well through his story has made me feel even worse about what happened, to be honest," she admitted. "He had so much life to live."

A heavy silence fell between them then. Tom was the first to speak "Look Ali…what's done is done and we have to get past it and move on in the best way we can, just like you with your marriage I suppose. You can't give up on life, or love, just because you've been hurt. Life's too short."

On a sudden impulse Ali stood, reaching up to kiss him gently on the cheek. "I know," she said. "And thanks for reminding me."

Remembering that kiss as he walked toward the pub half an hour later, Tom touched his fingers to the place where her lips had been. It was the kiss of a friend, that was all he told himself. And that was how it had to stay.

WHEN TOM ARRIVED at The Fisherman's Inn Lily was waiting impatiently, jumping from foot to foot like a five-year-old. She beckoned to him to follow her round the back and he laughed. "What's with all the cloak-and-dagger stuff?"

Opening the door into the old back kitchen where the puppies were she gave him her most beseeching smile. "You know what you said about the puppies," she began. "About giving one to Ali, I mean. I thought perhaps it should be the freckled one with the brown patch over its eye. She liked it best when I brought her to see them."

"What?" Tom shook his head in exasperation. "You mean you've made me come all the way here just to say that...and what were you doing bringing Ali to the pub?"

Lily stared at him defiantly. "What's wrong with that?"

"Well...nothing really I suppose, it's just...you know how Ned is about her. I wouldn't want him to start a scene if he bumped into her here, that's all."

"We didn't go into the pub," she insisted. "I told you we just went to see the puppies. You said she could have one."

"No I didn't say that," Tom corrected her. "I said I'd think about it."

Lily smiled imploringly. "Pleeeease Tom, she's so lonely."

"And what makes you think that she's lonely?"

"I can tell…you know, by the way she is. A puppy would take her mind off it."

"Off what exactly?"

"Off everything I guess," Lily said, splaying out her fingers. "Bobby…the accident…her husband."

For a moment Tom hesitated, needing to know. "Does she talk to you about Bobby?" he asked.

"Sometimes… He was in love with her you know."

Tom's heart tightened. "And how do you know that?"

"He told me," Lily said. "And he said that she didn't love him back yet but he was working on it."

Tom tweaked her nose. "Why is it Lil?" he asked. "That people always seem to talk to you?"

She looked at him wide-eyed. "Because I ask them. I asked Bobby if he loved Ali and I asked her if she loved him."

"And what did she say?"

"That he was just her friend. Please give her the freckled puppy, Tom."

"What…you mean now?"

"You could take it on your way home, as a surprise. They are eight weeks old after all and I've got puppy food and everything."

Ten minutes later, wondering how he'd managed to get himself talked into agreeing to Lily's plan, Tom headed back to Cove Cottages with the freckled pup in a fleece-lined bag in his arms and a bag of puppy food slung over his shoulder.

He saw Ali as he walked toward the row of cottages; she was standing right at the edge of the bay, so close to the water that it lapped over the toes of her boots. Her hands were thrust deep into the pockets of her bright blue duffle coat as she watched the tide come rushing in. A late seagull screamed overhead, a pale shape against the vast navy sky, and as he watched and waited uncertainly the full moon soared above them, turning the sea to silver. Ali turned and looked at him and in that moment she, too, was rimed with silver, like a magical ethereal being.

He walked toward her, holding her gaze with his, "I've brought you a present," he said, feeling totally out of his depth. "Although to be fair it was Lily's idea."

"If it was Lily's idea then it must be a good one," she replied with a sparkle in her eyes. "Come on then, let's go inside and you can show me what it is."

They walked in awkward silence toward the cottage, side by side. Tom glanced across at her, wishing he hadn't let Lily persuade him into this; it was one thing for him to help Ali with her research but surprising her with a puppy was personal and they'd already crossed that line once today. She probably didn't even want a dog anyway, and he'd vowed to himself not to let his guard down again; there was still way too much blame and pain around for either of them to really know how they felt. They needed to keep their distance and bringing her a puppy was a stupid idea.

"Well…?" Ali asked as they walked into the kitchen. "Come on…what is it?"

When Tom placed the bag carefully down on the kitchen table Ali watched with interest. Suddenly it rolled as the pup moved inside and when she let out a surprised cry he smiled, reaching inside to gently retrieve the little creature. The pup stared out at him with button-bright eyes, whining softly, and he immediately handed her over to Ali.

"Oh you little love," she cried, cuddling the bundle of fluff in her arms. "You are so cute."

"I take it you like her then," Tom said, feeling pleased with her reaction.

"Wouldn't anyone?" she cried, taking the pup between her hands and lifting it up to her face. "When Lily showed them to me this was the one I liked best… I take it she's yours?"

"Actually," he said. "She's for you. Lily got it into her head that you were lonely and you needed something to love."

"Do you know that your sister is the most caring and considerate person I have ever met…but how can I look after a puppy…even one as cute as Freckles?"

"Well you've named it now so I guess you'll just have to find a way to look after it. Lily's sent a bag of puppy food for you and, knowing her, probably a list of instructions for caring for it, too."

"But what will I do with it if…?"

"If what…?"

"Well I'm kind of in between things really aren't I? I mean, I left here after…after Bobby, because I didn't think I had any right to be here but then I decided that writing my book, would be a good thing so I came back. When it's finished I guess I'll have to go back to the city and my job as a journalist."

"And is that what you really want?" The serious note in Tom's voice threw Ali, and he almost regretted the question.

"I don't know," she murmured. "I don't know where I am or what I want anymore."

"And you can afford to take this time out?"

She nodded. "My dad left me some money. As you know I came here originally to write an article about fishing for him…it just feels as though I need to do it for

Bobby now. I'll do the article for my dad later. I'm sure he'd understand."

"Look, I think it's great the way you've chosen to keep Bobby's memory alive with your fisherboy's tale. It's a lovely idea. You need to just live for now though and let the future look after itself… Keep the pup, Lily's right, it'll take your mind off things."

"Thanks," Ali said with a warm smile, "for making up my mind for me." To his surprise she reached up again to give him a peck on the cheek.

Tom raised his eyebrows. "This seems to be becoming a regular occurrence," he said.

Ali laughed, shaking her head. "It was just a thank you kiss that's all… So are you taking a puppy, too?"

Tom shrugged, feeling warm inside. "I don't know. I'm thinking about it and Lily's a good persuader. Pip, their mother, is my dog really and I miss her, but she prefers to be at the pub and she loves Lily so I don't really mind. It would be nice to have one of her pups I guess… It's a big commitment though."

"You should do it," Ali told him. "I can help care for it and we can take them for walks together. It'll be spring soon—we can walk them along the shore."

"We'll see," Tom said, already looking forward to it.

CHAPTER FIFTEEN

IT WAS WELL over two months since she came back to
Jenny Brown's Bay, Ali realized, looking at the calendar
on the kitchen wall; two months of writing, two months
of trying to sort through the confusion in her head and
over five months since she and Jake had finally split up
for good. The last couple of weeks had felt like a real
turning point though, thanks to Freckles.

At first she thought she'd taken on too much when, lost
and lonely, the pup just hadn't seemed to settle.

"If you need someone to love then here I am," she told
the little creature, and then she'd sat down with Freckles
in her arms and talked to her for what seemed like hours,
about love and life and loss, all the things that had turned
her life on its head.

After the first few sessions of bonding Ali noticed
that she herself felt much more calm and serene, as if
opening her heart to the pup had helped to heal her, too.
Freckles had stopped whining and pining and they'd become friends, forever friends. In fact she couldn't imag-
ine her life without the little dog in it. Reaching down
she scooped the pup into her arms, holding her close.

"You," she said, "are the best thing that's happened to
me in a long time…and today we are going to take our
first proper walk with your brother."

Half an hour later when she stepped outside into the
fresh morning air, gulls were already circling in the sky

above the clifftop, their distinctive, haunting cries rising on the wind that buffeted the crooked trees. She'd come back here just after Christmas, filled with trepidation and doubts, but now it felt as if there was a whole new brightness to the sky, a promise of spring that brought fresh hope and lightness into her heart.

"And that's thanks to you," she told Freckles, attaching her new collar and lead before picking up the little dog. "And Lily of course," she added out loud. Tom had helped with her healing, too, but that thought she kept locked deep inside; they were friends, finally, and that was more than she thought they could ever be.

He approached her now as she walked along the shore. He had his pup on a lead but progress was slow as the fluffy white bundle didn't seem to quite know what to do.

"I didn't know if you'd come when I left you the message," he called, smiling. "It just occurred to me that now I've decided to have a dog again it would be nice for Snowy here to have a friend to keep him company on our walks."

Ali shrugged, trying not to look too enthusiastic. "I'm glad Lily talked you into taking him," she said. "You won't regret it. Freckles is the best thing that's happened to me in a long time and she'll love having Snowy around."

"I'll say," he responded as the little white dog suddenly raced toward Freckles, totally forgetting that he was still on the lead. When it jerked him to a halt he pulled back against it, frustrated at being constrained.

"It does look as if he'll need a bit more training on the lead though," Ali said, unable to contain a giggle. "Come on girl," she said to Freckles. "Let's show him how it's done... Or maybe not," she added as Snowy managed to wrap his lead around Tom's legs, almost making him lose his balance.

Suddenly they were both laughing together like two old friends.

"This is nice," she said as they sorted out the leads and set off again. "No pressure."

"No pressure is good," Tom agreed but there was a longing in his eyes as he looked at her. "It's nice to see you laughing again," he added.

"And you," she agreed. "Although if I'm honest I have to admit that it makes me feel...oh I don't know, a bit guilty I suppose."

They walked side by side, shoulders almost touching, as he took in what she'd said. "You should never feel guilty about laughing," he told her. "Bobby wouldn't have wanted that."

"Would he have wanted us to be friends?" she asked.

Tom nodded. "Of course he would. Is that what we are then...friends?"

"I hope so," she said with a smile.

Ali thought about their walk as she curled up in her bed that night. It really did feel that finally they were becoming friends; it was nice, she decided, and at least it was a start.

A start of what, asked her inner voice, what did she want it to be? Closing her eyes she pushed the question aside, refusing to address it... They'd walked along the shore that's all, had a few lighthearted laughs, talked dogs and remembered Bobby. It was enough for now and more than she'd expected.

FOR TOM, SLEEPLESS and confused, things weren't quite so clear. He couldn't look at Ali without his pulse quickening; the glint of gold in her hair when the sun caught it, the way her warm brown eyes crinkled at the corners when she smiled…and the inner glow she seemed to radiate. Everything about her drew him in however hard he tried to blank it out, and he couldn't get rid of the gut-wrenching guilt about his feelings. Today though, maybe because of the pups, it had been different; it felt as if they were both finally moving on as friends. He liked that feeling and he was determined not to mess up. They'd even discussed taking the dogs onto the shore again tomorrow, nothing definite, just a vague suggestion dependent on the weather. He hoped the weather would be good.

Sunday morning dawned bleak and gray. The sea seemed to merge with the sky with no distinct horizon, and storm clouds hung heavy in the air.

"No walk today," Tom told Snowy, who was standing near the door wriggling his whole body in anticipation… "Never mind, after breakfast we'll go to The Fisherman's and see the family."

It had surprised Tom to find how easily he'd adapted to having a companion around all the time; he talked to the pup constantly, airing his views and plans as if the little creature could understand his every word.

"Do you know," he said, reaching down to scratch behind the pup's ears, "I didn't realize how lonely I was until you came along."

Snowy whined in response and Tom laughed. "Are you disappointed about missing our walk with your sister? Well I'm disappointed, too, but don't worry, we'll call in there on the way past."

When he reached Ali's door with the pup carefully tucked inside his waterproof jacket, Tom hesitated. Should he just leave it until later? As he stood dithering on the doorstep the door opened and there she was.

"I suppose you've come to tell me that our walk's off." she said. "The pups are still too young to get cold and wet I know...you could stop for a coffee though. If you want to that is."

"Thanks," Tom said, a warm glow settling inside him. "I guess the kids can play inside."

"You've certainly taken this puppy ownership seriously." She laughed, ushering him into the kitchen. "Although I admit that at times it does feel as if I've got a baby to take care of."

Tom placed Snowy gently down on the floor, then watched the two pups playing. "Do you ever regret it?" he asked. "Getting Freckles I mean?"

"No of course not," cried Ali. "In fact I owe Lily for persuading you to give her to me."

Tom gestured in the direction of the window. "Well you can thank her now if you like because I can see her walking along the shore."

Not bothering to knock, Lily burst in through the front door and came running into the kitchen. "Oh," she said when she saw Tom. "So you're here."

"Well don't sound too pleased to see me."

"I am—it's not that... I wanted to talk to Ali about something."

"Don't worry, I know when I'm not wanted. Just let me finish my coffee and I'll be off... I was on my way to see Mum and Dad anyway."

Ali automatically held out her hand in objection. "No, it's fine, Lily. Anything you want to say to me you can say in front of Tom."

Lily's face turned a vivid shade of pink. "But it's Tom I want to talk to you about," she whispered.

Tom gulped back his drink and picked up Snowy.

"Don't worry I really am off... I'll call in on my way back, Ali...if that's okay?"

"Yes...sure," she said.

AFTER TOM LEFT, Lily turned toward Ali. "I want to ask you something," she said, her voice high-pitched with excitement.

Ali smiled. "...Yes?"

"Are you in love with Tom?"

Taken aback, Ali hesitated. "Why...no," she eventually managed. "Of course not."

"So do you still love your husband?"

Her response was instant. "No...definitely not."

Lily grinned with satisfaction. "There," she said. "You see."

"See what?"

"When I asked about Tom you went pink and stuttered but when I asked the same question about your husband you didn't hesitate."

"What's brought all this on, Lily?" Ali asked.

Lily pulled at her blond plait. "I heard Ned talking to dad."

"And what was he saying?"

"Ned said that you were after Tom, you lost Bobby and now you want Tom."

"And what do you think, Lily."

The girl's pretty face lit up with a broad grin. "I *want* you to fall in love with Tom," she said. "I'm sure he likes you."

Ali shook her head, moved by Lily's admission. "That's just wishful thinking I'm afraid. I don't think Tom wants a relationship with anyone, to be honest. His life is full enough with his fishing. And even if, as you seem to believe, he does have feelings for me, then I don't think he'd want to upset the rest of the family."

"It's only Ned who'd be upset. Dad told him that he needed to back off and get rid of all his bitterness. 'Bobby's gone,'" he said, "and we'll never forget him. We are still here though and we have to get on with living.'"

"And what did Ned say?"

"He just turned and walked off… So you will think about falling in love with Tom?"

"I hope you're not going to ask him the same question."

"I might…unless you tell me how you really feel."

"Look, Lil," Ali took both the girl's hands in hers. "I like Tom and I hope we're friends but love just happens. Sometimes you can't stop it even if you want to and sometimes you really *want* to be in love with someone but however hard you try it doesn't happen."

"Like that song," Lily cried. "You know…"

"What song?"

"I can't remember who sings it but I know some of the words."

"Go on then, let's hear it."

Lily took a breath and started to sing "I Can't Make You Love Me". Ali was dumbfounded.

"Oh Lily," she cried. "It's George Michael. That was so beautiful and yes…that's exactly what I meant."

Lily's pretty face puckered. "So you don't love Tom then," she said sadly.

"I don't love anyone in that way right now," Ali told her, trying to be totally honest. "I hope Tom and I are friends and maybe one day…who knows. But for now don't get your hopes up."

Ali thought about their conversation after Lily left, remembering the "moments" between her and Tom. The way his lips had felt against hers when he kissed her that day, warm and soft and so tender; it seemed so long ago now. The way her heart raced when she saw him. She hadn't been totally honest with Lily, she knew that now, but there again she hadn't been totally honest with herself either. She wasn't divorced and Bobby's death was still so raw… The timing just wasn't right…yet. One day though she really hoped it would be and until then…until then she had to take one day at a time. Finish her book, see a solicitor about the divorce…and maybe take out a longer lease on the cottage.

OVER THE NEXT FEW weeks Ali did just as she'd promised herself, taking one day at a time and seeing where life led her. She and Tom fell into a comfortable routine of walking the pups along the shore, more often than not accompanied by Lily, who brought Pip along, having been dissuaded by her mum from having one of the pups herself.

"Now that Tom has Snowy," she explained. "Pip really is my dog and I don't need two to look after, do I… Anyway I can always come and play with Freckles."

"Whenever you want," Ali told her. "You know you're always welcome."

Ali loved her walks with Tom alone, but having Lily along helped keep a distance between them. Somehow she knew that getting too close to Tom would probably be the quickest way to drive him away and that was the last thing she wanted. She also loved the time they spent working on her book, or rather she worked while he just talked. The moments when he dropped his usual guard and let his love of fishing and the sea take over were rare. She'd just sit and listen, sometimes taking notes but usually absorbing the atmosphere he created, storing it inside her head to recreate when she started to write.

"I remember the first time I took Bobby fishing on my own," he began one early evening in late March, after a brisk walk along the shore.

Ali sipped her coffee, watching the dogs play chase around the room and waiting patiently for him to go on; if pushed, he sometimes changed the subject so she just waited patiently and hoped he was about to expand on the story.

"It was about the same time of year as this," he went on. "I was about fourteen or fifteen so Bobby couldn't have been more than five or six. It terrifies me now to realize just how crazy I was then, to take a five-year-old out on a boat, but our parents were busy and it was my job to look after him for the day. I wanted to go fishing so I took him along in my little dingy."

He stopped for a moment then, recollecting the experience; his dark hair was curly with the damp spray from the sea and his cheeks were flushed from the bracing wind outside. To Ali he looked ruggedly handsome and more approachable than usual. Her heart did a slow flip as she remembered his kiss and for a second she closed her eyes.

"When we set off the bay was calm," he went on and she opened her eyes again, watching the expression on his face as he relived the moment and wishing that she'd known him as a young boy.

"We were around the point, near to a small island I liked to go to, when the wind came up. If I'd been a better fisherman then I'd have checked on the weather but I guess you just get on with it when you're fifteen. We'd caught a few little tiddlers. Bobby cried, I remember, when I made him put them back. He just kept shouting 'crabs, crabs, crabs.' It was all he wanted to catch. So to keep him happy I decided to row to the island and look for some there. I pulled the dingy up onto the sand, gave him a bucket to put his crabs in when he caught them and we set off on our search. He was so excited and we both totally ignored the wind, except for when I had to grab hold of him to stop him being blown into the sea.

"We walked for ages that day, around the edge of the large sand bank I thought was an island, stopping now and again to dig in the soft sand for crabs. Bobby found two tiny ones and he was pleased as punch. Then the rain started and I decided we'd better head back for the boat. By the time we got to where we'd left the dingy a full-blown storm had set in. Waves were washing all over the place and the dingy had disappeared. Bobby started to cry and I just yelled and yelled for help but no one came. We sat on the sand shivering with cold and wet right through to our underwear for what felt like hours. It was Bobby who spotted the dingy about twenty feet out. The sea had taken it but now it seemed to be blowing it back to us and there was only one thing I could do…"

"You didn't try to swim out to it, did you?" Ali gasped.

"Well I was about to," Tom said with a smile, "but Bobby was too quick for me—he just waded out and then suddenly he disappeared under the water. If he hadn't had his crab bucket with him I'd never have found him, but it bobbed up out of the water and I waded in to chest height, dragged him out and then retrieved the dingy. All he cared about was whether he still had any crabs left."

"And did he?" Ali asked.

"Fortunately he still had one," Tom told her. "Or he'd have cried all the way home. We never told our parents about that outing but I guess they'll know now when they read the book."

"Sure will," Ali said. "And thanks for that, it was a lovely memory."

Tom grinned. "I'm not so sure my parents will agree. It's kind of nice though to remember times like that without tears—stories about him growing up seem to bring him back to life…but in a happy way."

"Oh Tom," Ali cried. "That is exactly what I want the book to do."

"So do I get to read it now?" he asked, but she shook her head.

"When it's finished," she promised. "You'll be the very first person to read it."

After the shared emotion and closeness between them that evening Ali felt as if their relationship had moved to another level; she couldn't wait to see him again but to her disappointment he seemed to avoid her for the next few days. Determinedly she got on with her book, trying to focus on the words in front of her. Obviously their shared emotion that evening had frightened him off and she'd just have to live with that.

THAT EVENING WITH Ali had awakened him to feelings he didn't want to face. He was, first and foremost, a fisherman and he'd always said that he would never let a woman sit at home in trepidation, wondering whether or not he was going to return from his latest fishing trip. Bobby's drowning had not only strengthened that resolve, it had also made him feel even stronger about his passion for the sea. He felt that he owed it to his brother to keep their way of life alive. Otherwise what had he died for? Admitting to his feelings for Ali would serve only to confuse things even more. He needed to talk to her, to explain how he felt and make her understand.

Tom knocked on her door around eight thirty on a Friday evening, just as the sun was going down after a fresh, blustery day. She opened the door, greeting him with such a radiant smile that the breath caught in Tom's throat. Fresh from the shower, her damp hair curled around her face and her skin glowed with the warmth of the water.

"Hi," he said awkwardly.

"Hi," she responded, surprised to see him.

"I'm on my way home and I wanted to talk to you… the lights were on."

She held the door open, standing back to let him through. "Coffee?" she asked heading for the kitchen, "Or would you rather have a glass of wine?"

He shrugged. "Whatever."

"Wine it is then," Ali said, walking over to the cupboard for two glasses.

"Let me," Tom insisted.

He lifted the glasses down from the top shelf and then hesitated. She was still standing in front of him, so close that he could feel the heat of her body. She turned to face him, looking up to meet the intensity in his dark eyes, and all his good intentions were forgotten.

"Oh Ali," he murmured, lowering his lips to hers.

After placing the glasses down he took her in his arms, holding her hard against his chest as his lips finally claimed hers. She kissed him with such warmth and softness that he never wanted to release her. And when he finally, reluctantly, let her go, she reached up to stroke his cheek. "I'm sorry," he said. "I came here to talk to you, to be honest, and…"

Curling her hand around the back of his neck she drew his lips down to hers again, cutting off his sentence. "Perhaps this is you being honest," she murmured. "And don't be sorry."

It was Tom who pulled away first. "What happened

to the things you said, Ali, about wrong timing and taking one day at a time?"

"Impulse overcame good intentions."

He took hold of both her hands in his, gripping them tightly. "What just happened Ali…was it a sudden impulse, two confused people reaching out… Or was it more than that?"

She stepped away from him, reluctantly pulling back her hands. "I don't know…perhaps you should go now."

"Do you want me to?"

She shook her head, still holding his eyes with hers. "No… I don't. I just think it might be best, that's all, you know, to give us both a chance to think."

"No wine then?"

"Better not."

As he walked past her toward the door he stopped midstride, taking her arm and pulling her toward him again. "Tomorrow then," he murmured, brushing his lips against hers again as if daring her to forget. "Tomorrow I want you to tell me how you really feel."

"Tomorrow…" he heard her murmur as the door closed behind him.

CHAPTER SIXTEEN

AFTER TOM LEFT Ali's head was all over the place. What had just happened? What was she thinking? Then again, why not? They were both free and single. It was over five months since Bobby's death and she had nothing to be ashamed of. After all, no matter what Ned thought there was never anything more than just friendship between her and Bobby. The guilt was still there though, dragging her down. If only she'd realized how Bobby felt about her maybe she could have handled things differently. And despite everything, would Bobby really begrudge her and Tom happiness... Knowing him, somehow she didn't think so.

Leaning back in her chair she allowed herself to dream; *did* she and Tom have something special, she wondered, maybe even a future together? Oh how she hoped so, for her feelings for him made a mockery of what she thought she'd felt for Jake; back then she'd just been playing at love. So did she love Tom? The answer was too scary to contemplate. Besides, her divorce hadn't come through yet, her future was vague and she didn't have time for love, she told herself, already doubting her own dream.

Waking from sleep the pup, Freckles, pulled at her fluffy slippers with its needle-sharp teeth and she laughed, scooping the little creature up into her arms. "Well you certainly know how to bring me back down to earth with a bump," she said, walking down the hallway to take her outside. The painting on the wall near the door seemed to jump out at her, as if she'd never really seen it before. She stopped to look at it, remembering the story Lily had told her just the other day, about Ali's landlady, Elsa May Malone Evans; seemingly she'd found love in Jenny Brown's Bay and then she thought she'd lost her love, Bryn Evans, when he was swept away by the sea. That must be him in the painting, throwing a stick for a yellow dog way out on the huge expanse of sand while a woman with gold-streaked curly hair was watching from the shore…and the woman must be Elsa. According to Lily she'd found him again eventually, her Bryn, but not before she'd had a baby right here in this cottage.

Something rang in Ali's head…a jolt of recognition. She'd been so busy and stressed lately that she hadn't even thought about her period. Of course she had always had been erratic, and with all the stress of her split from Jake it wasn't really surprising that it had been a while since she'd had one. Then again she had missed taking her birth control pill a couple of times, she remembered with a surge of panic. It was during the emotional time after she'd accused Jake of seeing someone else and he'd managed to talk her round. Walking outside into the clear crisp air she put Freckles down, trying to remember how long it had been since she'd had her period; it must be well over five months, she realized, and that was worrying, even for her, especially since she'd felt so tired lately…

Sleep evaded Ali that night; she tried to relive those moments with Tom but they felt like a lifetime away now. All she could feel was a tingling fear and a fluttering anxiety that held her heart tightly in its grip. There was only one thing to do, and that was to go to the chemist in town as soon as possible; she had to put her mind at rest before she saw Tom again. Jumping out of bed she glanced at the clock. Eleven thirty, would there be anywhere open now? Asda, that was it, they were open all night.

It was weird, thought Ali half an hour later, walking around the quiet store in the middle of the night. A group of teenagers were giggling together by the doors, a couple with a baby were wandering sleepless and bleary-eyed around the children's section and an elderly man, looking lost and sad, was reading a paper. She quickly selected a pregnancy testing kit from the variety on offer, thinking that she must be mad and tomorrow she'd be laughing about it.

She drove home too fast, wanting to put her fears to rest so that she could let Tom back into her heart. *Tomorrow*, he'd told her. *I want you tell me how you really feel.*

This couldn't be happening, it really couldn't, and how could she have been so naive?

Freckles whined with delight when she let herself back into the cottage, but for once she ignored her, running straight up the stairs to the bathroom. The clock in the hallway said one forty-five. Before 2:00 a.m., she told herself, this nightmare would be over.

One fifty-eight and she stared at the stick. It seemed to take forever…and then, suddenly it changed and her whole world changed, too… Pregnant! She must be over five months pregnant and she hadn't even suspected. What a fool she was…and what to tell Tom.

By morning, she was sleepless, worried and confused. She stood naked at the mirror as the first light of dawn filtered into her room, running her hand across the mound of her stomach. Why hadn't she noticed it before, that new swell? And as she pressed gently down against it she felt a movement, just a gentle flutter but enough to know. It didn't matter what she wanted anymore; this was going to happen and it was her responsibility.

Something twisted inside her heart as she thought about Tom. Last night she'd asked herself if she loved him and now she knew; the answer was yes, but she couldn't do anything about it. She'd just keep this to herself, she decided, until she'd manage to get her head round it. At the moment it seemed like a crazy nightmare. She'd have to see a doctor, too, and put the whole thing into motion. It might be scary but it was going to happen no matter how she felt about it; she was going to be a mum; she, Ali Nicholas, a real mum. A prickle of excitement cut through the fear.

ALI RANG THE doctor at eight thirty and arranged an appointment for ten o'clock. One and a half hours to kill... and what if Tom called in the meantime; what would she say?

As it happened he knocked on her door at nine fifteen, just as she was about to leave. She peered out at him from an upstairs window. *Tomorrow you are going to tell me how you really feel*, he'd said, believing that he already knew. And he did know, she just couldn't admit it now. Holding back her tears she sat on the bed, frozen with fear and doubt. What if she just told him, what would he think? He knocked again, harder this time and tried the door, standing back to look up at the windows when he realized it was locked. Was she imagining it or were his shoulders slumped with disappointment when he walked away?

HEADING DOWN TO the small harbor where *The Sea Hawk* was docked, Tom went over the events of the night before again and again, reliving every moment. He'd tried Ali's door but it wouldn't budge. Where could she be…walking Freckles? No, that couldn't be it; she never locked the door when she just went for a walk on the shore. Disappointment and doubt flooded in as he turned away. What if she'd changed her mind, what if he'd misread the situation. He hadn't misread the look in her eyes though. He knew he hadn't. She felt the same way he did, he was certain of it, but where was she now?

Common sense prevailed; perhaps she'd needed something from the shop. After all, they hadn't really arranged a time for today… *Or she might be having doubts*, said an inner voice, a voice he tried to shut out.

"We'll call in later," he said to the little white pup that wriggled and squirmed in his arms. "Today I am going to introduce you to the love of my life…a beautiful sturdy vessel that's never let me down. You need to get your sea legs you know, if you're to start coming out with us."

As Tom approached Ned, he was happy to see a smile on his brother's face for once. "Bit young yet to be a fisherman isn't he?" he called from the deck of *The Sea Hawk*.

"Got to start somewhere," Tom responded, pleased to see his brother looking more carefree again. He and Ned were finally getting some kind of normality back—or as much normality as they could manage after the tragedy of losing Bobby. When Ned found out about him and Ali, Tom knew that his bitterness would kick off all over again and he wasn't looking forward to it. But there was nothing definite yet so they might as well enjoy each other's company today.

ALI WALKED INTO The Station House doctor's office filled with trepidation.

She stared with surprise at the small blond woman

who sat on the other side of the desk. The woman's youthful looks lent Ali no confidence at all. "Er…" she began awkwardly, looking around expectantly. "I have an appointment with a Doctor Moss…"

The woman smiled. "Yes…that's me. I am Doctor Moss. What can I do for you?"

Ali sank down into the chair opposite. "I'm pregnant," she announced. The words made it seem so real that she felt the beginnings of panic. "At least… I've done a test, two tests in fact."

"And both were positive."

Ali nodded, too emotional to speak.

Doctor Moss smiled gently, noting her consternation. "And I take it this has come as a shock?"

"Just a bit… My husband and I split up over five months ago."

The doctor scribbled notes down on her pad. "And is your ex-husband the father?"

Ali nodded again. "He doesn't know yet but the baby definitely is his."

"Okay," Doctor Moss looked at Ali, and for one panicky moment, Ali wondered if the doctor knew who she was. Jenny Brown's Bay was a small place, after all. She might have heard the rumors about Bobby's death. But the doctor merely motioned her through to a small side room.

"If you'd just like to slip out of your things in here and pop the gown on I'll give you an examination. We'll need a urine sample, too, but we can get that later."

Lying on her back on the examination table, feeling nervous and uncomfortable, Ali almost grabbed her clothes and ran.

Doctor Moss was quick to return from her preparations. "Now," she said in a calm voice. "You don't need to worry. Just relax as much as you can and it will be over in no time."

The examination was embarrassing, uncomfortable rather than painful and thankfully soon over. Ali hurriedly dressed and returned to sit opposite the doctor, trying to take deep, regular breaths.

Doctor Moss looked up from her notes, smiling warmly. "Well," she said. "You are definitely pregnant and everything seems to be as it should."

Ali nodded. "I feel like such a naïve fool. I've had so much going on though and my periods have never been regular. I just didn't realize... So what now?"

"I do still want you to go and give a urine sample today. Nurse Kate will show you where to go. I'll make an appointment for you with a midwife and you need to see a consultant for more tests. I'll put all that in motion today and you'll probably get an appointment at the hospital very soon since you are so far along with your pregnancy. Have you noticed any movement yet?"

Ali nodded. "Just a kind of fluttering feeling really."

"That's fine. And any pregnancy symptoms...nausea, cravings..."

"Not that I've noticed."

"And do you have any questions or worries?"

Ali gave her the ghost of a smile. "Plenty of worries but no...no questions."

"And you are in a position to deal with all this? Do you have any support?"

"Yes..." Ali lied, biting her bottom lip. "I'll be fine."

"Well you're young and healthy," the doctor said, holding out her hand, "so there's no reason why everything shouldn't be very straightforward... If you do have any worries though don't hesitate to call me."

Ali took hold of her proffered hand, wanting to cling

on to it but instead she shook hands briefly and smiled. "Thank you," she said. "I will."

Back home, in the cottage, Ali sat with the pup in her arms, trying to take in the fact that she really was pregnant; her whole life was about to change dramatically, again, and there was nothing she could do about it. She'd just go on as she was. It was the only way—tell no one in town and say nothing. People would find out soon enough, that was for sure, and she'd deal with the curious looks and tittle-tattle then…but what to tell Tom?

Her heart tightened and a heavy misery swelled inside her. Today he wanted to know how she really felt about him; what was she going to say? She couldn't avoid him forever.

The day dragged on. Every sound made Ali jump. Her whole being was tuned in to the sound of his voice calling her name, his knock on the door. And when it came she panicked, just as she had in the morning.

TOM WALKED SLOWLY homeward with the pup under his arm. They'd had a good day, he and Ned, even talked about stuff from the past. They were finally getting back to some kind of normality and he was about to break it did he really want that? He should probably back off with Ali, explain the situation; she'd understand. The way his whole body shivered with longing when he thought about her said differently.

"I don't know, Snow," he said. "What do you think I should do?" The pup whined in response and he scratched the backs of its ears. "What was that, boy?" Snow whined again, louder, and he laughed. "Ah, so you think the same as me. Okay then we will call in again on our way home."

Her car was there, he could see it in its usual parking place. With a surge of anticipation he knocked three times. No reply. She had to be in…surely. "Ali!" he called through the letter box. "Ali! What's going on? At least speak to me."

When he thumped on the door again it slowly opened, just a crack. "I'm sorry," she whispered.

Tom pushed his foot into the gap. Her face was pale and strained looking, tears streaked her cheeks. "Ali," he cried. "What is it?"

"I'm sorry," she said. "I… I can't do this."

"What, Ali? Do what?"

She wouldn't meet his eyes. "Us," she cried. "I can't do us right now."

When he tried to take her in his arms she pulled away from him. "I'm sorry, Tom," she cried.

"But why?" he groaned, feeling as if his heart was being torn out.

"It's the wrong time… Please…you need to go now."

The door shut and Tom found himself walking away from the happy future he'd thought lay ahead of him.

"Oh Snowy," he murmured when the little dog reached up to lick his chin as if in sympathy. "What do I do now?"

He already knew the answer to his question, and by the time he'd reached his own front door he admitted it to himself. He had to back off and keep his distance for a while, and who knew…maybe their time would come eventually. One thing was for sure; after she'd made her feelings so clear he wasn't going to start chasing after her. The sad thing was that he'd really believed her answer to his question was going to be very different.

CHAPTER SEVENTEEN

IT WAS MIDAFTERNOON by the time Grace Roberts and Lily had finished the lunchtime rush. Grace smiled as her daughter hurried to dry her hands and take off her apron.

"Can I go now, Mum?" she asked.

"It depends on where you're going," Grace said.

Lily shrugged, looking sheepish. "Just to take Pip for a walk."

Grace raised her eyebrows. "To see Ali Nicholas I suppose?"

"Might be," Lily responded defensively.

"Oh Lil, I know you too well for you to try and pull the wool over my eyes. I don't mind you seeing Ali, I've already told you that. Just don't be too long and be careful on the road."

"I'm always careful," Lily insisted. "I'm not a kid anymore, you know, Mum."

Grace's round face puckered. "I know love, you'll be eighteen very soon and that's grown up."

Watching her daughter, as she walked off down the road with Pip running along beside her on a lead, she couldn't help but sigh. Lily might think she was all grown up and she had to let her believe that. Truth was she would always be a child and Grace would never stop worrying about her until the day she died.

AT COVE COTTAGES Ali was trying to concentrate on writing but her thoughts were all over the place. In a couple of days she had an appointment for her scan and no one but she would see the picture of her baby growing inside her; it made her feel so alone that she wanted to cry. In fact she felt tearful quite a lot lately.

Since she'd spoken to Tom that day he'd done as she asked and stayed away. Trouble was she really missed him, but how could there ever be anything between them when she was having another man's child? She had far too much time on her hands, time in which to brood and speculate on her loneliness and worry…and on what might have been. Come to think of it, the only person she'd really seen since her doctor's appointment, apart from the woman who worked in the village store, was Lily.

Without Lily keeping her head straight these last few days, popping in on a regular basis to see Freckles and chat about normal things, Ali didn't know what she'd have done. Even Lily was becoming curious, about the secretive way she was behaving.

"You look worried, Ali," she'd said a couple of days earlier and, "You look so tired. Are you ill?"

For a moment Ali had almost broken down and told Lily the truth; to be able to share her troubles would be such a relief. Instead she'd just complained of a headache, which hadn't seemed to convince the girl at all. Just yesterday Ali had caught her staring at her with a speculative expression, as if trying to work out what was going on. Lily may be different but she wasn't stupid, it was only a matter of time until she worked it out for herself, and she'd be so hurt to find out that Ali hadn't trusted her with her secret.

A knock on the door brought her from her reverie. Pip

raced through to greet the visitor and for just a moment Ali's heart lifted; could it be Tom?

"Ali," called Lily from the hallway. "Are you in?"

"Come through," Ali called. "I'm in the kitchen."

Lily appeared in the doorway with Pip at her heels, stopping in the doorway and stepping nervously from foot to foot. She looked so young… Beneath her thick quilted jacket her slim legs, encased in black woolen tights, seemed too skinny to support her, and with her long fair hair tied back neatly into two plaits she could have passed for a twelve-year-old.

"Are you all right?" she asked.

Ali forced a smile. "Of course I am. Why wouldn't I be?"

"Because there's something wrong with you," Lily said determinedly. "And I can always tell when there's something wrong with people."

"Well you don't need to worry about me," Ali announced, jumping up to put the kettle on. "And this time you're wrong, I'm afraid… Do you want tea?"

"Juice please," Lily replied, watching with a curious frown as Ali moved around the kitchen. "You've got fatter," she said bluntly.

Ali stopped, wrapping her arms self-consciously around her body; the self-control she'd been carefully nurturing disintegrated and tears oozed from her eyes as she sank down onto a chair. "I'm… I'm having a baby, Lily, but it's got to be our secret."

Lily's face lit up with excitement. "But that's brilliant," she cried. "So why are you crying and why does it have to be a secret? Everyone will know soon anyway because they'll be able to see, and isn't it supposed to be good news, finding out that you are having a baby?"

Ali dropped her face into her hands. "I don't know,

Lily. It may sound terrible but it doesn't really feel like a good thing to me. In fact, to be honest, I don't know what to think. I didn't know myself until a few days ago and it's come as a shock… I… I've got a scan in a couple of days. Please don't tell anyone though…not just yet."

"Does Tom know?" Lily asked.

Ali shook her head. "I haven't told anyone so no one knows…except you."

Lily smiled. "I like that. I like us having a secret. When will it be born?"

Placing her hand on her belly Ali stroked it gently. "Not for a while yet," she said thoughtfully, then she looked up at Lily. "Will you come to the scan with me?"

"Come to the scan," Lily repeated in awe. "Me?"

"I can't think of anyone else I'd rather have there."

"Is that when they take a picture of the baby in your tummy?"

Ali nodded, waiting for her answer. When it came she breathed a sigh of relief, feeling that she wasn't totally alone.

"I'd really, really, love to come," Lily cried. "Can I tell Tom? He's good at secrets."

"No!" A surge of panic flooded over Ali. "I don't want you to tell anyone."

"Okay," Lily agreed, "but what shall I tell Mum?"

Ali thought for a moment, not wanting to encourage her to lie. "It's at ten o'clock the day after tomorrow so why don't you just tell her that we're going to take the dogs out somewhere, and we will take them with us in the car so we are telling the truth."

Lily grinned. "That's clever. Mum says I must never lie to her. 'Me and Ali are taking the dogs out somewhere,'" she repeated as if trying to keep the words in her head, and then she jumped up and went across to where Pip was playing with Freckles. Clipping on her lead, she headed toward the door. "I have to go now," she said reluctantly, "but I'll come back to see you to-morrow...oh and, Ali?"

When she stopped at the door Ali smiled encouragingly. "Yes?"

"Who's the baby's daddy?"

"Why..." Heat rushed up Ali's neck, flooding her cheeks. "My husband of course... Jake."

"But I thought you liked Tom."

"I do...like Tom. Of course I do. It...it's complicated."

"So are you going away soon then, to live with him again?"

Ali shook her head, wondering how to explain it to someone who saw things as simply as Lily. "No," she said. "I'm staying here. We tried to give our marriage another chance but it didn't work out."

"And you got pregnant."

"Yes, stupidly, I did, but I've only just realized it."

"So can I still come with you to see the baby's picture?"

"Of course you can."

Lily nodded happily, heading for the door again. "That's all right then," she said.

"And don't forget," Ali called after her. "Not a word to anyone."

Lily turned back to look at her, her fingers pressed firmly against her lips.

To Ali's disappointment Lily didn't show the next day, and she almost wished that she hadn't broken down and shared her secret with someone so young. To ask Lily to keep something from her mother wasn't fair. She almost expected Tom to come hammering on her door, asking questions, or even Ned; he was sure to think that the baby was Bobby's.

The day passed uneventfully, however, dragging relentlessly by. Ali watched for Tom on his way to work and back, longing to speak to him, but he didn't even look in the direction of her cottage as he walked past.

"Oh Freckles," she said to the bright-eyed little pup whose zest for life and neediness motivated her to get up and go outside into the fresh air. "What would I do without you to keep me busy?"

The day of the scan dawned bleak and gray, reflecting Ali's mood. She ate sparsely, forcing down some toast. It looked like she was going to have to go on her own after all, she thought, watching hopefully for Lily.

She was ready to set off and was just settling Freckles in the back of the car when, to her delight, Lily finally arrived. Her normally pale face was pink with exertion and today she wore lipstick and a bright blue dress that made her look very grown up.

"Sorry I'm late," Lily called. "Shall I put Pip in with Freckles?"

"Oh yes…" Ali said. "To be honest I thought you weren't coming."

Lily stopped and looked at her quizzically. "And were you happy or sad?"

"What…about you coming with me to the hospital, you mean?"

"Were you happy?" Lily asked again. "When you thought you were going on your own?"

Ali smiled. "What do you think?"

"I think I'd have been very sad if you'd gone without me."

"And I was very sad when I thought you weren't coming…now jump in and let's go get this baby's picture taken."

Lily chattered endlessly all the way to the hospital, about how she'd helped her mum bake cakes yesterday and how the pub had been so busy at lunchtime that she hadn't been able to call in on Ali. "Tom was there all day, too," she added.

"What?" Ali asked. "Making cakes you mean?"

The idea brought a gurgling giggle up Ali's throat and Lily let out a snort.

"No…of course not, he was doing some business with Dad and Ned. I think it was to do with Bobby because they all looked very sad… I didn't tell him about the baby but I wanted to. He'd probably help you if you told him, you know."

"I don't want him to know about the baby and I don't need any help," insisted Ali. "Except from you of course," she finished, relieved to see a smile replace Lily's hurt expression. "I really didn't want to come here on my own."

The hospital maternity unit was busy; women ranging from teens to early forties waited patiently, cradling their bulging stomachs. Finally a young nurse holding a clipboard called out, "Ali Nicholas."

FOR LILY, SEEING the baby's image on the screen above the bed where Ali lay was magical. Ali stared at it in awe, moved to the core by the reality of the child she carried.

"Do you want to know the gender?" asked the nurse.

Ali glanced across at Lily, who nodded in excitement. "Yes," she said. "Yes please."

"Well," said the nurse. "As far as I can tell, and remember it can never be one hundred percent certain… you are having a little girl."

Lily squeezed Ali's hand when she saw the tears in her eyes.

"A girl," Ali repeated. "I'm having a girl."

ALI LEFT THE hospital feeling as if she was walking on air.

"That was amazing," announced Lily, dancing round in circles. "Please can she be called Daisy?"

"We'll see," Ali promised, already trying out the name in her head. Daisy... She liked that.

Before dropping Lily off outside the pub, Ali reminded her yet again not to say anything.

"But you'll need people to help you," Lily insisted. "You can't have a baby all on your own and I don't really know what to do."

"Just for now," Ali promised. "And then we'll see."

ALI HADN'T BEEN home for half an hour when the euphoria began to fade. Seeing the baby had been magic but the reality was tough and she needed to face up to that. The quiet of the cottage brought home the fact that she was very much alone; if she had problems there was no one to turn to.

Her thoughts began to go wild; what if something happened in the middle of the night? What if she went into labor? She'd gotten herself into this situation by being totally irresponsible and now it was time to face up to it. Picking up her phone she scrolled down to Jake's number; should she ring and tell him that he was going to be a father? He could take on a part of the responsibility.

Clicking the phone off she closed her eyes tightly; no good doing things on impulse. She needed time to think her actions through. He was her baby's dad but he'd always insisted that he never wanted kids; this responsibility was hers for now.

Four thirty and the afternoon light was beginning to fade. Bobby's face kept slipping into Ali's mind, making her realize once again just how much she missed him; he'd been such a good friend to her, listening but never judging, really caring how she felt. She just wished that she'd been as understanding of *his* feelings. On a sudden impulse she pulled on her coat and settled Freckles in her bed. Perhaps being near to him would help her get things more straight in her head. Walking hurriedly out of the cottage, she headed along the shoreline. There was a shortcut to the village along the cliff path.

Ali climbed the steep slope wondering if she was being ridiculous. She'd been visiting Bobby's grave on a regular basis since she came back to Jenny Brown's Bay and she often just sat and talked to him. Today though the soothing peace of the graveyard brought no comfort. "I'm so, so sorry, Bob," she murmured. "For not knowing."

Someone had put fresh daffodils on Bobby's grave, flowers that spoke of hope and spring and new growth. She touched them gently, thinking that for Bobby there was no hope, no life…thanks to her selfishness and lack of perception. "Oh Bobby," she murmured. "I'm so…so sorry." And then her head was in her hands and the tears she'd been trying to keep in check were running down her face in a river.

CHAPTER EIGHTEEN

TOM WALKED QUICKLY through the village, eager to collect Snowy from the pub and get home to Cove Road after an eventful fishing trip that had ended with few fish but a whole lot of work to do on *The Sea Hawk*'s engine. As he passed by the beautiful old village church, where yew trees and holly grew by the gate in rich shades of green, his thoughts turned inevitably to Bobby; if his brother had been here to help then maybe they'd have caught more fish before the engine started playing up. Now they'd have to go out again as soon as possible.

The sun was low in the sky and long shadows fell across the grass. It was a peaceful place to be laid to rest, he thought, looking in the direction of Bobby's grave over in the far corner. He froze. Someone was there, standing by the headstone. He'd left Ned at the boat, his mum and dad were at home and he'd just spoken to Lily on the phone five minutes ago… So who was it? Ali…did she visit? For a moment he hesitated, torn between going to check and staying away.

It *was* Ali, he realized, recognizing the lonely looking figure by the far wall. When she dropped to her knees and let her head fall into her hands, all his good intentions about keeping his distance were swept aside.

He approached quietly from behind her, his heart aching at her obvious pain. "Ali," he said, placing his hand on her shoulder.

She swung round to face him, her cheeks damp with tears. "Tom!"

Without conscious thought he took hold of both her shoulders, forcing her to look at him. "What's up?" he asked, his voice gentle. "Is this about Bobby?"

When she didn't answer he took hold of her hand. "Come on," he said. "Let's walk."

They walked in silence. Her hand felt good in his, warm and soft and…right. "I'm sorry if I pushed you too quickly," he said. "I should have clung on to our friendship for longer and not frightened you away by pushing you too fast."

She shook her head, withdrawing her hand. "No…you don't understand… I…"

"What…what don't I understand?" He took hold of her again despite her resistance, drawing her close but not quite touching, afraid of moving too fast again. "Look," he suggested. "Let's make a fresh start, no blame and no regrets. We can be friends again, can't we, and then… who knows where that might go?"

Her whole body trembled beneath his touch. "You don't understand," she cried.

"What?" he asked. "What don't I understand? Tell me, Ali, please."

She looked up at him, her soft honey-brown eyes brimming with tears. "I'm pregnant, Tom… I'm going to have a baby."

Tom felt as if something was clawing at his guts, as if everything about her was a lie. How could his instincts be so wrong? "Bobby's?" he had to ask, his voice cold and hard.

Her shoulders tightened against him. "How could you even think that?" she cried, pulling away from him. "You, of all people… I trusted you but that trust was obviously misplaced."

The accusation in her eyes was like a physical blow. But before he could recover or say anything, she turned and ran, out of the gates and into the road.

Tom watched her go, frozen to the spot. In the moment when it most mattered he'd let her down. "Ali!" he yelled after her. "I'm sorry."

He followed her slowly, his head going around in circles. Pregnant! She was pregnant…and if it wasn't Bobby's then who was the father? Jealousy gripped him, bringing a rush of anger; he needed to know. For a moment he wanted to run after her, to grab hold of her, tell her he was just a jealous idiot and ask her for the truth. He'd revealed his doubts about her and Bobby, though, doubts he had kept deep in his subconscious, when believing in her had mattered most; she'd never forgive him for that. But why shouldn't he have doubts? Only a few days ago he'd really believed that he was falling in love with her and that she loved him back, when all the time there had been someone else. He wanted to believe that it wasn't Bobby's, did believe it…but it must be months since she and her husband split.

Hardening his heart and nursing his pride he turned back toward pub Collecting Snowy from the, where he'd left him in the care of his mother, was more important than chasing rainbows. Perhaps he'd had a lucky escape.

ALI DIDN'T STOP running until she reached Cove Road. She'd been dreading the day that Tom found out about the baby but the reality was worse than her fears. She knew he'd be angry and hurt and jealous; she'd imagined it so many times in her head, talking him round, explaining how she and Jake had given their marriage one final chance before she'd found out Jake had no intention of remaining faithful to her. That Tom would think the baby might be Bobby's had never come into the equation. She'd really believed that he trusted her, but instead he'd suspected her all along, and somehow that made him no better than Jake. Now she was lost and lonely and scared of the future.

Opening the front door she was greeted ecstatically by Freckles. "At least you don't judge me," she said, grateful for the pup's attention, and then she felt it, the rolling, fluttering sensation she'd experienced previously but stronger now. A feeling of well-being came over her, and she clasped her hands to her belly with a surge of newfound strength.

"It's just you and me now, Daisy," she said, savoring the name on her tongue. "And you are what counts in all this…nothing else matters now."

Freckles whined softly and she smiled. "And you, girl, you matter, too. Three girls together…come on, I'll get your tea."

TOM'S FOOTSTEPS WERE slow and labored as he walked toward The Fisherman's. Spring sunlight shone on the weatherworn building, showing its cracks and faded paintwork. However hard his dad worked to try and keep the place looking nice, the wind and spray from the bay soon battered all his efforts. A family were coming out of the pub, mum, dad and two giggling youngsters. They clasped hands, laughing as they ran toward the shore, and Tom felt more isolated than ever. Until he met Ali he'd been content, happy with his own company, and his fishing of course. She'd made him want more, and now it was too late to go back…and the worst thing of all was that he'd really meant it when he told her he believed her about Bobby. Yet all the time, deep down, he'd been lying to himself.

"Hi, Tom, have you come for Snowy?"

Lily's light, melodic voice brought him sharply back to the moment and he looked up to see her standing right in front of him. "I… Yes," he muttered, stuck for words.

She frowned. "Are you okay?"

He tried to smile but Lily knew he didn't mean it. "Of course…" he said. "I'm just tired I guess."

Lily took hold of his hand, urging him toward one of the wooden tables outside the pub. "No you're not," she insisted, sitting down beside him with concern in her eyes. "Is it because of the baby?"

"Baby?" he repeated. "What do you know about a baby?"

She placed her forefinger to her lips, glancing left and right. "It's a secret," she whispered. "Mine and Ali's secret so don't tell anyone."

"What do you know about the baby?" he repeated.

"I know that Ali has just found out she was pregnant and she hasn't said so but I think she's scared of people finding out."

"Because people might think it's Bobby's you mean," Tom said, as he had.

"Oh no, it's not Bobby's baby," Lily insisted.

"Then whose is it and how do you know anyway?"

Lily smiled. "I asked her…like you probably should have done. I guess by the expression on your face that you've screwed up."

Tom dropped his head into his hands. "Oh Lily," he groaned. "She was upset and when I asked her what was wrong she broke down and told me she was pregnant."

Lily sighed. "And what did you say?"

"I asked her if it was Bobby's."

"She'll never forgive you, you know," Lily pointed out. "She trusted you. She thought you believed her... about Bobby, I mean."

"I thought I did, too," Tom said, "but I just had this huge rush of jealousy and I thought she must have been making a fool of me all along."

"Well she wasn't...the baby is her husband's. They tried to give their marriage another chance but it didn't work out. I think it was ages ago. She didn't mean to get pregnant, you know, in fact she said it was stupid."

"I can't believe that I'm asking you this," Tom admitted. "But what do you think I should do now, Lil?"

Lily shrugged, but she seemed pleased that her big brother was asking her advice. "Talk to her, Tom. Be a friend and be honest. How can she trust you when you only pretended to believe her?"

"So what you're saying is that I have to prove myself," Tom said. "But I don't know anything about babies."

"Just be nice, Tom," Lily said "And see what happens."

As Tom walked home with the pup tucked under his arm he went over and over his conversation with Lily. He really had thought that he was falling in love with Ali, that maybe they even had a future together, but that future hadn't covered someone else's baby. Truth was he was scared, scared of letting her down again with his doubts and scared of the responsibilities that being with her now held. He'd always said that he'd never put his wife through the fear of being a fisherman's wife, much less a child. And did he really love Ali? he asked himself honestly. The answer was instant. Yes...yes he did love her, but was it enough? Could he love another man's child?

Surprisingly Tom slept deeply and heavily that night. Overcome by emotions and the problems of the day, his body just shut down. He woke as dawn crept in through his window; and he lay on his back looking out at the sky, remembering yesterday. Ali was having a baby, another man's child. Even if he did do as Lily suggested and try to be a friend to her, would she want that, and would he be able to cope with all it entailed? He figured the best thing to do for now was to stay away from her until her initial hurt and anger faded…and until he could get his head around the whole thing.

IT WAS EASY for Ali to tell herself to be strong and put the baby first; the reality in the cold light of day was not quite so simple. It was scary and very, very lonely. Lily was her only friend and she couldn't put too much of a burden on her.

Maybe she did need to tell Jake. The baby was his daughter after all and it was only fair to let him know he was going to be a father. As she clambered out of bed to go and see to Freckles, her resolve faltered. Jake had never wanted children, so why would he choose to be involved now? No way was she going to have her daughter rejected by her own father.

The morning dragged; she watched Tom walk past her window on his way out and she almost opened the door and called out to him, but what was there to say? When he stared straight ahead without so much as a glance in her direction she realized that she was wasting her time. She had to get over him, to focus on her and the baby's future; she'd immerse herself in her writing, get Bobby's book finished before the baby came and then maybe just move on.

Lily arrived after lunch. "How are you?" she asked. "And have you seen Tom?"

"I saw him walking by without even a look in my direction," Ali said.

"Talk to him, Ali," Lily suggested. "Stop him on his way home and make him listen."

Ali shook her head. "I have nothing to say to him, Lily. The first thing that came into his head was that the baby must be Bobby's. That means he's never really trusted me, no matter what he said, and I'm sure, deep down, that he still doesn't."

"But what did you expect him to think," cried Lily. "He didn't know that Daisy was your husband's...and to be honest, even if did, he'd still have been jealous."

Suddenly Ali smiled. "I just realized what you said."

"What?"

"You called the baby Daisy."

"Well it feels like a Daisy." Lily clutched her hands together. "Oh please call her Daisy."

"Daisy Nicholas," Ali said slowly, trying it for size. "It does have a nice ring to it."

"If you married Tom you could call her Daisy Roberts and she'd be like my sister."

"Oh Lily." Ali gave the girl's shoulder a quick squeeze. "That's a lovely idea but don't go getting your hopes up. Anything that may have been between me and Tom is long gone, I'm afraid... I do think I might call her Daisy though."

"That's brilliant," shrieked Lily.

At least she'd made Lily happy, Ali thought.

THE DAYS RAN into weeks and spring gave way to the promise of summer, bringing warmth and color to the world. Despite Lily's efforts, Tom and Ali determinedly kept their distance from each other.

Ali had convinced herself that she was better off on her own, even though she was lonely. She was still hurting deep inside, but she tried to focus all her attention on finishing her book. The story was drawing to a conclusion along with her pregnancy. Soon her baby would be born, that was certain, but the ending of the book evaded her. It was meant to be a reflection on Bobby's life, a story that would keep his memory alive…a happy read. To even touch on the tragedy would destroy that, so she was toying with the idea of ending the book with him going off to college. It might feel sad perhaps that he was the first of his family to do something other than fishing but his life and hopes and dreams would still be ahead of him. It would be a positive way, a happy way, for his family to remember him, she thought.

She cried as she wrote his story but they were happy tears, and that was what she wanted the readers to experience. The fun he and his brothers had together, the scrapes he got into growing up as he learned his trade as a fisherman…and the love he and his family shared.

The baby had been growing inside her for over six months when she wrote the final chapter, and on that day, inspired by the idea of family and feeling very alone, she picked up her phone and called Jake.

WITHOUT BOTHERING to knock Lily burst through Tom's front door. "Tom… Tom!" she yelled, hurrying through the hallway and into the kitchen.

His muffled voice floated down from upstairs. "In the shower, Lily… I won't be long."

Snowy bounded toward her and she sank down on her knees to cuddle him. "Bet you're missing Freckles," she said. When the pup looked up at her, head tilted and long pink tongue hanging out the side of its mouth as if he understood, Lily laughed out loud. "Don't worry, boy," she told him. "We'll find a way to get them together, you'll see."

Five minutes later Tom ran down the stairs drying his hair with a towel. "Okay," he said, well aware of Lily's attempts at matchmaking. "What is it now?"

"I want you and Ali to be friends again. She needs help."

"Lily..." He shook his head, looking affectionately at his sister. "I'm fond of Ali, you know I am, but she's having a baby with her husband and they need to sort out their differences; I'm sure they'll soon get back together now."

"But she doesn't love him anymore and anyway he doesn't want to know," she told him. "When I called in just now I heard her crying, and then she started yelling on the phone."

"What did she say?" Tom asked, intrigued despite his reservations.

"She said 'I should never have rung you. It was a big mistake and I don't want you to have anything to do with her anyway so just forget it,'" Lily told him.

"Oh Lily," Tom said with a sigh. "When are you going to learn not to go interfering in people's lives and jumping to conclusions? You don't even know that she was talking to her husband?"

Lily practically quivered in frustration. "I am not jumping to conclusions," she cried. "Honestly I'm not, and it *was* her husband she was yelling at. He made her cry... Oh, and by the way, she's finished Bobby's book, you know."

For a moment Tom froze, emotion flooding through him. "She promised me that I'd be the first to read it when it was done," he said, remembering.

"Well then ask her," Lily suggested. "She can only say

no and it must be at least two weeks since you spoke to her so it'll give you an excuse."

"I'll see," Tom promised. "Maybe tomorrow. Now you need to get off home. Mum will be worried…and, Lily."

"Yes…"

"Stop worrying about Ali. I'm sure she can look after herself."

CHAPTER NINETEEN

AFTER LILY LEFT Tom couldn't get the information she'd given him out of his head. So Ali's husband didn't want anything to do with the baby; if that was true then what was she going to do now? Lily also said that Ali had finally finished Bobby's book without letting him know. Despite their differences he'd thought she might have told him; she had promised that he'd be the first to read it. Perhaps he should just go and talk to her, as Lily had suggested. But if she said no it would make the situation between them even more difficult than it was now. No, he decided, a promise was a promise and her book was about Bobby after all; he had a right to read it.

She answered on his second knock and as the door swung open anticipation flickered inside him, overcoming his doubts.

"Oh... Tom," she said, nervously pushing a stray lock of hair back behind her ear. Then she stood aside, motioning him in. "Are you looking for Lily?"

"Lily...er...no," he responded. "I just... Lily said you'd finished your book."

Ali nodded. "I've sent it to a publisher friend of mine to see what he thinks."

For a moment he hesitated, feeling hurt and annoyed. "But you said you'd let me be the first to read it," he reminded her.

He looked tired, Ali thought, tense; it made her heart

ache. "I wasn't sure if you'd want to read it now after... you know."

"After what?" he asked.

She shrugged awkwardly. "Well we've hardly been getting along well lately, have we. It's been weeks since we've even spoken."

"A promise is a promise," he insisted. "No matter how the situation has changed."

"I know that, I just didn't think you were interested anymore."

He held her gaze, raising his eyebrows slightly. "Interested in you, do you mean?"

She felt her cheeks flush. "No of course not," she snapped, annoyed with herself for rising to the bait but unable to help a sudden rush of anger. "I just didn't think you were interested in the book that's all."

"But why wouldn't I be?" Tom responded. "After all it is about *my* brother."

"Oh yes," she said, her voice distant and cool. "The brother you thought I was sleeping with."

"Look, I..." he began. He seemed to hesitate for a moment before turning abruptly and walking out.

"Tom," Ali called after him, wishing she'd kept her mouth shut. Okay, when he'd asked her if the baby was Bobby's it had really hurt, but bearing grudges and making sarcastic comments wasn't helping anyone. Tom was entitled to his own opinion and she couldn't blame him for thinking the worst. Everyone else surely would.

"Just forget it," he responded without looking back.

It was almost dark when Ali placed a copy of Bobby's book in a plastic bag and slipped out of the door.

The night air was cold and a blustery wind blew in from the sea, lifting her hair in a tangled cloud above her head. She clasped her arms about herself, looking out across the dark shimmering water. Way out in the bay she could see the lights of a fishing boat, a stark reminder of her one tragic fishing trip. She gripped Bobby's book tightly, remembering. What if Tom refused to read it or what if he hated it; what if she'd got it all wrong?

She could see him through a crack in the curtains; he was sitting quite still staring into space. Oh how she wished she hadn't made that cheap remark; placing the plastic bag carefully on the step outside his front door she knocked twice before hurrying off.

TOM CLOSED HIS eyes, going through their stupid conversation; if only he'd been more civil. He was hurt that she'd finished the book without telling him and then sent it off for some stranger to read about Bobby's life before he did; his impulsive question about Bobby being the baby's dad had obviously hurt her a lot, and the crazy thing was that until the words had left his mouth he'd really thought he trusted her. Deep down though he hadn't or the thought would have never come into his head. So did he trust her now, he asked himself? Did he even know? Perhaps she was right to be so angry and disappointed.

He heard a sound at the door, breaking through his reverie. A knock? He went to see what the noise was, throwing open the front door only to have it pushed back in his face by the wind that was howling across the bay. Grasping the handle firmly he peered out into the semi-darkness. Ali's lights were on, he noted, warm and bright in the black night; was it Ali who'd knocked, he wondered, or had the wind just hurled something against his door?

When the moon slid out from behind a dark cloud its pale light picked out a movement from farther along the shore. Was someone there? "Hello," he called, stepping outside. "Hello."

The only response to his call was the high-pitched moan of the wind and he turned away from the stormy night, eager to get back inside. His foot hit something on the step and he stopped in surprise to see a plastic bag shining in the moonlight; picking it up carefully he felt the weight and shape of it in his hands, his heart lightening. So it had been Ali.

Closing the door behind him, he put the bag on the table and carefully withdrew the manuscript, staring down at the title that leaped out at him.

A Fisherboy's Tale.

For Bobby.

Tom read Ali's words with a sense of amazement; laughter came alongside pain, and the joy in the pages made him feel as if he was on a roller coaster of emotion that left him breathless. The stories she told of Bobby as a boy growing up in the shadow of his two brothers were so real that he couldn't understand how Ali had gleaned so much information. Of course when she first came to Jenny Brown's Bay she'd spent a lot of time talking to some of the older fishermen who frequented the pub; it had all been just about the fishing back then but she'd absorbed the atmosphere of the place and they were sure to have told her tales about the Roberts boys.

She'd also taken in everything he'd told her in their early chats, and when he'd called round in the evenings; she must have a real way of drawing people out because he couldn't even remember telling her some of the stories in the book and they had to have come from him. Like the day when, after being told off by their dad, ten-year-old Bobby had decided to run away to sea; Tom had followed and found him looking for a fishing vessel to stow away on. He'd explained to Bobby there were only local fishermen in the bay, and persuaded him to come home, promising he wouldn't tell a soul.

And then there was the tale Tom had told her about five-year-old Bobby fishing for crabs on the mysterious sand bank island that wasn't mysterious at all; tears brimmed as he relived that day as if it was just yesterday, feeling every moment. Every antic Ali recounted brought pain and a terrible sense of loss but also so much joy. He recalled the laughter they'd shared when they were walking the dogs along the beach and he'd told her about the caves that were revealed only at low tide. He, Ned and Bobby had decided to go and search for the treasure that they'd heard was stowed away in the caves. It could have gone horribly wrong when they'd almost got trapped, but as usual they'd escaped by the skin of their teeth. That story had made Ali laugh, he remembered now, reading about it in the book. She was good at laughter, wholehearted and spontaneous; he liked that.

It was the summer he turned fifteen when they searched for the caves and the treasure; Ned was eleven and Bobby must have been only six. Whatever had he been thinking to put his younger brothers at such risk? It was the last time though. The following year he'd left school and become a proper fisherman, way too old for kid's adventures, or so he'd believed.

After that the stories Ali told were unfamiliar; they were about Bobby and Ned and latterly Bobby and Lily. In one incident, if it was true, Bobby had taken six-year-old Lily to the small island around the headland that was supposed to be haunted by Old Bill, an elderly fisherman with a long white beard. If you saw him it was said that you'd have good luck with your fishing for ten years. Bobby and Lily had crept around the island and started screaming when they thought they saw Old Bill. He turned out to be a white goat that must have some-how managed to get onto the island at low tide. Bobby and Lily had then corralled the goat onto their boat and set it free on the mainland.

Now where had Ali heard about that, he wondered. From Lily he'd guess. In fact most of the rest of the tales had probably come from Lily: after all she had spent most of her life either listening to her brothers talk about their exploits or being directly involved herself. Most of the stories were slightly exaggerated of course but they were all based on fact and inspired by Bobby's life. She'd used the real names too; he liked that.

The main thing that came through, was Bobby's char-acter, that fun-loving, high-spirited character that they all loved and missed so much, beautifully portrayed by Ali. She'd managed to show his serious side, too, his pride at catching his first fish, his efforts to become as good at fishing as his brothers, his love of the sea and the life they all led. And as Tom read the final pages while the pale light of dawn crept over the horizon, he wept with both sorrow and joy for a life well lived but for way too short a time.

CHAPTER TWENTY

ALI SLEPT RESTLESSLY, wondering if Tom was reading Bobby's book. What if he hated it, what if he thought all the facts were wrong, what if he thought it didn't do his brother justice?

She'd stored up so many bits of information, from Tom and from Lily, and Bobby when he was alive. At first she'd been writing about fishing as a way of life, listening to the fishermen who went into the pub in the evenings. Each and every snippet of information she'd carefully stored up, either on bits of paper or just inside her head. By going through it all again and again she'd gradually formed a picture of Bobby as a boy and she'd tried to tell a truthful tale of a special young man.

Tom's approval of her book, Bobby's book, meant so much to her. They may not have a future together now but her feelings for him were as strong as ever. She needed to cling to her pride, though, so he would never know that.

Trying to put her apprehension about the book from her mind, Ali grabbed a piece of toast, drank down her cup of breakfast tea and reached for Freckles's lead. "Come on, young lady," she called.

The pup ran eagerly toward her, and after snapping on the lead she headed out of the front door into the fresh morning air. All traces of last night's turbulent weather had disappeared. The sea was tranquil, sparkling in the summer sun, and the gentle, rhythmic swish of waves upon the shore brought Ali a whole new sense of peace. Inside her belly Daisy kicked, making her jump, and she laughed out loud, counting her blessings. For now at least she lived in an amazing place, she had no money worries and the baby she carried was healthy and strong. Her book was finished and it was time to focus on preparing for Daisy's birth. At the moment she had only herself to take care of; but once Daisy arrived she'd be half of a "we" and she'd never really be alone again. She liked the idea, she decided, heading along the shore with the sea breeze in her face.

She'd walked only for a few minutes when she saw a man approach. At first glance her heart began to race; was it Tom? As he came closer she drew back. It was Ned, walking toward Cove Cottages. Her thoughts raced and her breathing quickened; should she say hi or should she just ignore him? Maybe she could simply nod and scuttle by.

As he came alongside her he hesitated. "Hi," she said, hoping friendly was the best approach.

He glared at her. "I need to know the truth."

Dismayed by his show of aggression but feeling that she owed him, Ali stopped. "What do you mean, Ned? The truth about what?"

He looked her up and down, focusing on her baby bump. "About the baby. It's Bobby's, isn't it."

Anger soaked up her initial alarm. "This baby is mine," she insisted, wrapping her arm protectively around the familiar bump. "And it has nothing to do with your brother whatever you might like to think."

As she tried to walk past him he stepped in front of her, blocking her path. "Well I think you're lying," he said determinedly.

The ferocity of his accusation brought a vague shiver

of apprehension but her anger overrode it. "The trouble with you, Ned," she announced, looking him straight in the eyes, "is that you can't read people and you jump to conclusions without thinking things through. I don't have to defend myself to you anyway. You're just soaked up by bitterness and jealousy and that's sad."

"How can I not feel bitter when my brother died because of you?"

"And you're saying that it was my fault?"

For a moment Ned hesitated. "Well you did make him bring you here—and you put us all against each other by insisting that you come out on the boat that day... He was in love with you. It was obvious."

Seeing the pain in his face Ali hesitated, her anger draining away. "This baby isn't Bobby's, Ned," she told him. "Maybe you're right and he was in love with me, but if that's true then I certainly didn't know it. If that makes me selfish then I'm sorry, but Bobby and I were just friends as far as I was concerned...good friends."

Ned frowned, going over their conversation in his head. "So why did you say I was jealous?"

His question shook her. When she'd blurted out the words it had been on impulse, to hurt him maybe. For a moment she thought about it. "Just an observation I suppose," she eventually said. "I'm a journalist—it's my job to notice things about people."

"Pity you didn't notice how Bobby felt then," he snapped. "And who do you think I'm jealous of anyway?"

"Well, your brothers of course, but don't get me wrong, I'm not saying that you don't love them. It's just..."

"Just what?"

"Well," she replied cautiously. "As the eldest son Tom has always been in charge, I suppose. It was obvious to me right from the start that you resented that slightly.

You went against him that day on the boat remember and backed Jed and Bobby about me coming out with you."

"I wish I hadn't," Ned muttered.

"Also," Ali went on, ignoring his quip, "Tom has always been the one your dad listens to, despite the fact that you work with Search and Rescue. It was different for Bobby—he got away with anything he wanted because of his charm, but I think you sometimes felt left out."

"Well you're wrong about that," Ned insisted, his face turning a dull red. "And I do love my brothers, always have."

On impulse Ali reached out and touched his arm. "I know you do," she said, softening toward him. "There's always jealousy with siblings though, that's just how it is. It doesn't mean you don't care about each other."

"And did you care at all?" he asked quietly. "About Bobby. Or were you just using him?"

Ali drew back her hand. "Of course I cared about Bobby…just not in the way you think. And I wasn't using him."

"Well if that is true and he really isn't your baby's dad then who is? Tom…is it Tom?"

"Don't be ridiculous," Ali snapped.

Ned shrugged. "Or maybe you're lying to all of us and it really is Bobby's baby. After all he isn't here to tell us the truth is he."

"But why would I lie about that?" Ali insisted. "After all it would be quite convenient to have your family's backing and you'd never know the truth, would you."

"Have you never heard of DNA tests?" Ned said. "All you have to do is fill in a form online and send some money. They'll supply the stuff you need to take a swab from the inside of your mouth and hey presto, it's as simple as that. And it doesn't even have to be you—anyone who has access to your baby could do it."

Ali stiffened, biting her tongue to keep back an angry retort. "I don't need a DNA test to know who my baby's father is," she said, holding her head high as she started to walk away. "And it's no one else's business so I suggest you just back off."

Several yards on she couldn't resist glancing back to see if Ned was still there. To her surprise he was standing motionless, watching her retreat. Did he believe her about Bobby? she wondered; somehow she didn't think so. Someone had managed to make Tom doubt her credibility, no matter what he said, and she didn't need to look very far to guess who that might be. Ned Roberts had a lot to answer for and he was obviously hurting more than anyone realized.

Ali walked to the headland, waiting patiently while Freckles investigated the scents and sights that surrounded them. As she headed back toward the row of cottages that sat at the very edge of the shore a dull, nagging pain settled across her back and she felt a wave of weariness wash over her.

"I think I've overdone it girl," she said, reaching down to scratch the pup's ears. Or was it just her unpleasant confrontation with Ned that had caused the dip in her spirits.

Reaching the front door of Number Three she pushed it open and went inside, heading straight into the sitting room to collapse on the sofa. She'd lie down for a bit she decided, that should sort her out. She just needed a rest.

EVER SINCE HE finished Ali's book Tom hadn't been able to put it out of his mind; it had really brought Bobby back to life for him and he couldn't wait for his mother to read it. He needed to go and see Ali though, he knew that, for no matter what their differences were right now, the book united them and he wanted to tell her that.

When he stepped outside he saw her at once. She wore a blue floral dress that fluttered around her legs in the breeze as she walked along the shore with the pup on a lead. Someone was coming toward her, walking quickly with long purposeful strides. Ned—it was Ned. Whatever was he doing here? For a moment Tom froze, apprehension looming inside him. Was he planning to speak to Ali? Well if he was then it wouldn't be to say anything pleasant; he'd been complaining about her for weeks, ever since he found out about the baby.

For several minutes Tom watched helplessly, not wanting to interfere. He could see that they were both animated and he was worried about Ned upsetting her, but then she just turned and walked away with her head held high; he admired her for that. Ned stood and watched her go; he looked angry, and Tom wondered if he should go over and speak to his brother. Ali walked slowly away from him, seemingly unperturbed by their confrontation, so Tom decided to keep a low profile and catch up with her about the book later.

She came back from her walk after just twenty minutes or so and Tom gave her time to go inside and get settled before heading over to see her, the manuscript tucked in the crook of his arm. He knocked on the door. "Hello… Ali!"

When he got no reply, alarm bells rang in his head. He pushed them aside; she'd probably gone for a shower or something. He'd come back later.

It was as he walked away that he heard the cry. At first he thought it was the scream of a gull but then it came again; it was human…a human cry.

"Ali!" he yelled again, more urgently now, running back to push open the front door. He burst through into the sitting room that overlooked the sea and stopped in the doorway, waves of panic rendering him helpless.

"Tom!" she called desperately, her eyes wide with panic. "The baby…it's the baby. It's coming…now."

"Right." He found his voice suddenly. "I'll ring for an ambulance."

"No," she begged. "There's no time. You have to help me now… I have to push."

"My mother then," he insisted. "I'll ring her. She'll know what to do."

"No… Please, Tom, it's…" she began and then she was gripped in a pain so intense that it took her totally in its grip. Her face contorted, tears squeezed from her eyes and she let out a loud cry of agony. Tom sank to his knees beside her, taking her hand as she started to pant.

"Breathe," he urged. "Just breathe."

As the contraction abated she let out a sigh. "You have to do it," she begged, her voice breaking as another contraction took her in its grip. "Help me, Tom… Please."

He raced up the stairs in a panic, desperately trying to think as he rifled through the cupboards until he found some towels. Rushing back downstairs two steps at a time, he spread the towels on the carpet beside the sofa and then carefully helped Ali ease herself down onto the floor and into a more comfortable position. As she lay back her pupils dilated and she clung to Tom's arm, stifling a groan.

"I have to push," she cried. "Now."

"Then push," Tom told her, adjusting her dress and calmly removing her panties. There was no time to think, no time for embarrassment; he acted on instinct, urging her again and again to push, watching and waiting while she gripped so hard onto his hand that her finger-nails drew blood.

"I can see the head," he cried, overcome by emotion. "Come on now, Ali...one really big push."

With a huge surge of energy Ali pushed, her face turning beetroot red as she gave it her everything. "It's coming," he yelled as the baby slid into the world.

Picking the baby up in his arms, Tom reached for a towel. She needed to cry, that was one thing he knew, though where the knowledge had come from he had no idea. Acting purely on instinct he gently rubbed the little mite, massaging her chest until she started to scream; healthy lungs delivering life. With a powerful emotion he'd never experienced before, gently and carefully he wrapped Daisy in a clean towel and placed her in Ali's arms, meeting her wide, proud, satisfied smile with one just as huge. "There you go, *Mum*," he said, automatically leaning down to place a kiss on her forehead. "Well done...and now I am going to ring the hospital."

TOM FOLLOWED THE ambulance to the hospital in his pickup, for who else was there to go, and anyway he told himself, he felt kind of responsible now.

When he saw Ali again she was sitting up in bed nursing Daisy. Her eyes were wide and soft and so filled with love that it made his heart hurt. "You okay?" he asked, wondering if she wanted him there.

She nodded, tears brimming. "Thank you," she said. "I don't know what I would have done if you hadn't been there to help me."

"You were amazing," he said. "And now you're a mum...awesome thought."

When he looked down at the baby's scrunched little face he found himself searching for Bobby's likeness and hated himself for it. "I'll come back tomorrow." He hesitated. "If you want me to that is."

She nodded shyly. What had seemed quite normal in the urgency of childbirth now made them feel awkward. "I'd like that, if you don't mind, and I'm sorry you had to…you know."

He shook his head, dispelling her regret. "I'm just glad I turned up at the right time… Is there anything you need by the way?" It felt like small talk, which seemed absurd given the situation.

"No…thanks." She held his gaze. "My bag, the one you collected for me, was already packed with everything I might need…please will you tell Lily."

"Of course…" he agreed. "She'll be so excited. Can I bring her to see you?"

Ali nodded enthusiastically. "You could come back tonight if you like. I'm not going to be in here long anyway."

"What…you mean they might send you home already?"

"That's what they told me, as long as the baby's okay. To be honest…"

When a flush ran up her neck, coloring her cheeks, he frowned. "To be honest what?"

"Please don't be annoyed but I think they presumed we were a couple and I didn't put them right because I wanted to go home as soon as possible… It's not as if I expect you to look out for me or anything so you don't need to worry. They've checked Daisy over and they say that for a preterm baby she seems really healthy, and as long as I have support then I should be able to go home very soon."

An unexpected smile flitted across Tom's face as her information sank in. "Ah," he said. "So they must think

that as I delivered the baby, then I must know what I'm
doing, when the reality is that I didn't have a clue."

"Now you tell me," she said, smiling back.

It was only as Tom was driving home that he realized he hadn't mentioned Bobby's book, or asked her
what Ned and she had been talking about. Both could
wait until tomorrow when Lily wasn't there, he decided,
wondering why he was so looking forward to seeing Ali
again. She'd just given birth to another man's child and
he was a long way from being ready to take on father-
hood; even if the baby had been his it would have been
daunting. He needed to take a step back and think about
this; he was prepared to help her out but he mustn't let
himself get sucked in.

He was attracted to Ali, he couldn't deny that, but
things were different now and he had to keep a strict
control on his feelings. Ali and he had had their moments; moments when he really thought they had a future together despite the fact that the odds were stacked
against them at every turn. Now though it felt as if way
too much water had passed under their particular bridge
for them ever to be more than just friends.

Parking outside the pub he hurried inside to find Lily.
To his dismay the first person he bumped into was Ned.

"You look a bit stressed," remarked his brother.

"So would you if you'd just helped a baby into the
world," Tom said with a ring of pride in his voice.

"Her baby?" Ned asked in surprise. "But I only saw
her this afternoon and she seemed fine."

"What did you say to her?" Tom's voice held an ac-
cusing note.

"I asked her what everyone else is thinking."

"And that is?"

"I asked her if the baby is Bobby's…and don't tell me you don't want to know."

Remembering that moment of birth when he'd looked at Daisy's face for Bobby's likeness, Tom froze.

"Everyone knows that when a child is first born it looks like its dad," Ned went on. "It's nature's way of making sure that the father accepts it, so they say… So go on, what did you think?"

"I think you should just shut up," said Tom coldly. "Anyway, I know for a fact that it's not Bobby's baby."

"Told you that, did she?" Ned raised his eyebrows, smirking. "You need to wise up, Tom. Bobby's gone so she's sweet-talking you now."

Without another word Tom pushed past his brother and went to look for Lily. He was shaking, he realized, holding out his hand. What was that all about? What was Ned's problem? He was helping Ali out, that was all.

CHAPTER TWENTY-ONE

As soon as Lily saw Tom she knew. "It's Ali, isn't it," she said, jumping up and down. "Has she had the baby?"

Tom nodded. "Yes, she's at the hospital and she wondered if you'd like to visit tonight."

"With you?"

He nodded, Ned's words ringing inside his head. *Bobby's gone so she's sweet-talking you now.* "Yes, with me," he said. "I just happened to call in when she was in labor and…"

"Oh my goodness!" Lily cried. "You mean you actually helped with the birth?"

"Didn't really have a choice," he admitted sheepishly.

"Come on then," she said, grabbing hold of his sleeve. "Are we going now? I'll need to stop somewhere to get her some flowers."

"I wouldn't bother," Tom told her. "She and the baby might be coming home tomorrow. You can get her some then."

Lily's face lit up and her voice rose in excitement. "Do you think she'll let me help her with Daisy?"

Tom smiled, infected by his little sister's exuberance. "I'm sure she will," he said.

WHEN THEY WALKED into the ward Ali was sitting in a chair beside the bed holding Daisy in her arms. In the moment before she looked up and saw them Tom experienced an unexpected and mind-blowing wave of tenderness, Never before had he seen such a glow on anyone's face, a glow of such love that it made Ali's skin appear almost translucent.

"Daisy!" cried Lily, and the moment was gone, but Tom knew that it would be etched in his mind forever.

He watched patiently while Lily cooed over the baby. It was strange now to think that he had actually helped bring the little mite into the world, actually held Daisy's tiny naked body and gently wiped it clean before placing her in her mother's arms. *Awesome* was the word that sprang to mind and even that didn't come close to how he felt about the whole experience. For a fleeting second Ali looked up and caught his eye, smiling softly in recognition of their shared bond.

"Thank you," she murmured. "For everything."

Tom shrugged, embarrassed by the warm feelings that welled up inside him. "It was nothing that anyone else wouldn't have done in the same circumstances," he insisted.

"Can I hold her, Ali...please," Lily begged.

He turned toward his sister, glad of the interruption.

"I think you'd better wait until she's a bit bigger, Lily," he suggested.

"It's okay, Lily," she said. "Here, you can hold her. I'll help you."

Lily seemed to enjoy every minute of the visit, but for Tom, it dragged on and on. He felt awkward in Ali's company when a short time ago they'd been friends...and it had nothing to do with embarrassment about seeing her give birth. It was more that he was acutely aware of her every gesture, the way she lifted her hand to make a point and the way her face lit up when she laughed. He needed to stay away from her because he didn't know how to cope with the feelings she brought out in him. They'd almost been way more than friends before he found out about the baby, and then he'd messed up by asking her if Daisy was Bobby's child.

He'd believed her, too, when she'd denied it but still he kept on looking for a likeness, as if something inside him wouldn't let it drop. Ned hadn't helped either, with his accusations. And then there was the bottom line; even if the feelings he harbored for Ali were strong enough to get over all that, there was still the fact that she came with a ready-made family; he definitely wasn't ready for that. Plus he'd always said that if he ever got married he would have to change his whole way of life.

As they said their goodbyes he felt sad to be leaving and guilt washed over him. He should have behaved differently, been more gracious. He could see the puzzled look in her eyes and his heart ached for her sorrow but still he couldn't bring himself to be open with her.

Lily on the other hand wore her heart on her sleeve. "Can I come again…please?" she asked, throwing her arms about Ali's neck.

"Well I might be coming home tomorrow," Ali told her, kissing her softly on the cheek.

When Lily asked if they were picking her up, a flush colored her cheeks.

"I'll probably get a hospital taxi," she said, glancing awkwardly across at Tom. "But you can come and see us whenever you want and—"

"No—" interrupted Tom, stepping forward. "You don't need to do that—just ring me when you know what time and I'll be here to drive you back to Cove Cottages… I presume that's where you'll be going?"

"Of course," cried Ali; a wide smile lit up her features. "Bring Lily with you if she wants…and Tom…"

"Yes..."

"Thank you. I realize that this is awkward for you but a lift home means a lot."

He gave a brief nod, wishing it could have been more but so afraid of taking that leap. "See you tomorrow then," he said.

"Tomorrow," she repeated. "I'll ring you."

As he drove Lily home, Tom's mind went back again and again to the moment when he and Lily had walked into the ward. Ali had thanked him, her eyes bright with emotion, and he'd been so ungracious. It was just panic, he realized. The whole situation had spiraled out of his control, and he hated not being in control. In the last twenty four hours there had been way too much raw emotion for him to handle.

"Daisy is beautiful, isn't she, Tom," remarked Lily in a dreamy voice, breaking his train of thought.

"Yes," he instantly agreed. "And Ali looked lovely, too, don't you think; motherhood must suit her."

Lily just looked out the window, smiling a happy little smile. "Well I think so," she said.

AFTER TOM AND Lily left, Ali sat in her chair with the baby on her breast, breathing in Daisy's distinctive scent, unable to believe how she could have turned overnight into a different person. Just a couple of days ago she'd had very little to do with babies and even worried that her mothering instincts might be lacking. As soon as she held Daisy in her arms for the first time, a huge rush of emotion had flooded over her, a suffocating wave of love that bordered on ferocity. This baby, this precious delicate child was an extension of her own being and she would do anything to keep her safe.

Somehow she'd known just what to do, holding Daisy

so naturally in her arms as she suckled, and glorying in the feel of her child drawing strength from her own body.

"You're a natural," the midwife told her. "Perhaps she'll be the first of many."

Ali shook her head firmly at that. "I don't think there'll be any brothers or sisters for a while I'm afraid," she responded with a smile.

"Of course there will," declared the midwife, Susan. "I saw the look in your partner's eyes; not many men would have been able to do what he did either, helping you with the birth like that. You're a very lucky young woman."

"But he's not…" began Ali, biting her tongue as she remembered what the doctor told her earlier, when she asked about going home. *When it's a first baby, and especially a preterm, I like to be sure new mothers have support at home before I agree to an early discharge. Although of course in your case I don't need to ask the questions as it's pretty obvious that you have a very capable partner.*

"So when do you think we'll be able to take Daisy home?" she asked.

"Probably tomorrow, depending on how the baby's doing. At the moment though everything seems fine. She's feeding well, you seem to have plenty of milk, and to be honest you seem to be taking this whole motherhood thing in your stride so…fingers crossed."

"Fingers crossed," repeated Ali with a beaming smile. "Hopefully I'll be ringing Tom first thing tomorrow then."

AT ELEVEN O'CLOCK the next morning Lily burst into the ward, her pretty face alight with excitement. "Are you ready?"

"Where's Tom?" Ali asked, cradling Daisy in her arms.

"He's just parking up in the short stay car park. I said I'd go on ahead to tell you that we were here. He's bringing the baby carrier."

A nurse Ali didn't recognize bustled over to make sure that everything was in place for Ali and the baby's discharge. "I'm Nurse Emma," she said. "All ready to go home, are you?"

Ali nodded, smiling with excitement. "Yes…as ready as I'm ever going to be."

The nurse nodded, understanding. "It's a big step when it's your first but you'll be fine. Now you do have someone at home to look after you, don't you?"

For a moment Ali hesitated, looking round to see Tom standing behind her.

"I guess that'll be me then," he said, looking uncomfortable.

"She can stay in for another night if you're not sure," said the nurse.

He shook his head. "That won't be necessary."

"Good…does she have everything she needs in place?"

"Yes…" cut in Ali. "We've left no stone unturned."

"Glad to hear it…now, enjoy your baby and call your midwife at once if you have any problems."

For Ali, walking out of the hospital with Daisy in her arms was the most bizarre experience she'd ever had. She wanted to go home, but she had no idea what she was doing. How dare the nurses let her loose with a newborn baby after just forty-eight hours? What if she messed up; what if she didn't have enough milk; what about cot death and choking?

"You're panicking, aren't you," Tom said, noting her consternation.

She nodded, holding back tears.

"Look…" He took hold of both her shoulders and made

her meet his eyes. "Women have babies every day and they cope. It's natural to be worried but it's also natural to care for your baby. Just follow your instincts and nature will show you the way."

She wanted him to take her in his arms, to hold her and stroke her hair. "You're right," she said, drawing away from him. "Thanks, I'll remember that."

"And Ali…"

"Yes…"

"I'm just two minutes away remember, so you're not really on your own when Lily and I have gone home."

"I'll be staying at least until teatime today anyway," added Lily. "And I'll be back first thing in the morning so you don't need to worry at all."

"Come on then," Ali said with a determined smile. "Thank you both so much and now let's go home."

To ALI'S DISAPPOINTMENT Tom didn't stay at the cottage for long. He brought in her bag, made a cup of tea for them and then announced that he had some jobs to do. "Mum needs you to be back at the Fisherman's by five thirty, Lil," he said. "I'm going over there later too so I'll call in here at about five o'clock; if you're still around then we can keep each other company."

After Tom left, Ali deliberately kept herself busy, feeding Daisy and then settling her down in her Moses basket.

"You look sad," Lily remarked. "Is it because Tom's gone?"

Ali denied it at once. "No…of course not… I'm just tired that's all."

"It was pretty cool though wasn't it, him delivering the baby and everything. Was it a bit embarrassing?"

"I didn't have time to think about it," Ali said slowly,

remembering how she'd yelled and groaned and how he'd had to deal with everything. He'd been amazing at the time but no wonder he was so distant now. It had been way too much for anyone, she could see that; from now on she'd just act normal with him and try to avoid any awkwardness between them. She may have blown any chance of a relationship with Tom but at least they might still be friends, had to be friends really after the way he'd helped her. And she had far too much going on in her life to worry about any of that anyway.

"Will you sit quietly with Daisy and maybe just hum to her while I nip to the bathroom?" she asked Lily. The pride in the girl's face as she started to hum made Ali smile; she wasn't alone in this so she didn't need to worry. She had Lily right there beside her and Tom keeping watch from a distance…it was a good feeling.

For the next week Ali just got on with learning how to be a mum and tried not to bother Tom. Lily came each day and Tom popped his head around the door each morning on his way to work and then again on his way home, just to make sure she was okay. If Ali felt disappointed about the briefness of his visits or the fact that he hadn't mentioned her book she managed to hide it, even from herself. She was just happy to have Tom keeping an eye out for her and he obviously hadn't gotten around to reading *A Fisherboy's Tale* yet.

Fortunately Daisy proved to be a happy, easy baby who cried when she was hungry and slept for the rest of the time. Lily was a godsend, helping in any way she could and getting in extra supplies Ali needed. She was grateful, but secretly disappointed that Tom didn't take more of an interest in her and the baby. He was kind to her, and he made sure they were okay, but nothing more.

Almost three weeks after Ali and Daisy arrived home

Lily announced that she was going away with her mum for a couple of days, to visit her aunt. Ali felt a rush of panic at the idea of her not being around but she didn't show it.

"Have a lovely time," she said when Lily came running in to say goodbye to her and Daisy.

"We will," Lily promised, hugging Ali so tightly that she could hardy breathe and kissing Daisy on the cheek. "I have to go now because we're running late. Mum's waiting in the car but she told me to say hi and I'll ring you three times a day."

"Make sure you do," Ali called after her as she ran down the path. "I'll be waiting."

As SHE WATCHED them drive away she found herself really hoping that Grace had told Lily to say hi to her. She used to get on so well with Grace Roberts and ever since the accident she'd really hoped for an opportunity to talk to her. The timing had never been right though, she still didn't really know how Grace felt about her, and the last thing she wanted was to cause the other woman any more pain. The whole family was still grieving and she wasn't even sure that she deserved Grace's forgiveness.

CHAPTER TWENTY-TWO

IT WAS MIDNIGHT when Ali woke, her head heavy with sleep. For a moment she just lay there, getting her bearings, remembering that Lily wouldn't be bouncing in today to help with Daisy; it made her feel lonely.

The night was black as coal with no moon to pierce its density. She lay on her back listening, overcome by the depth of the silence. Panic fluttered inside her—she couldn't hear Daisy breathing. She jumped up and reached for the bedside light; a warm glow filled the room, bringing reality back, and she exhaled.

Daisy was lying on her back in her Moses basket. Her eyes were closed tight and her skin seemed to have a waxlike gleam. She was pale—too pale—and her breathing was weak and shallow. Ali reached down and gently picked her up.

"Daisy," she murmured, her voice breaking. "Daisy! Mummy's here, sweetheart."

Cradling the baby's body against her, Ali reached for another blanket. Daisy's body felt so cold and yet her head was burning…what was wrong? "Daisy," she pleaded. "Come on, sweetheart, wake up…please."

When there was still no response Ali reached for her phone with shaking fingers to ring for an ambulance. But what if it took ages to come? Daisy needed to go right now, in the car, but she needed to hold her in her arms… to keep her warm. Tom, she had to ring Tom. He answered groggily, his voice thick with sleep. "Hello… Ali, is that you…what's up?"

Her voice was high-pitched with panic, and her words came out in a garbled rush. "Tom…oh Tom… It's Daisy."

He swung round to sit on the side of the bed. "Take a breath, Ali," he told her. "Just try and tell me slowly and calmly, what is wrong with Daisy?"

She gulped, trying to follow his advice. "I… I think she's ill. She needs to go to the hospital"

"Right," he said, taking control of the situation. "Just ring for an ambulance right now, I'll be there in a couple of minutes. Or better still, maybe we should just head straight for the hospital. Wrap her up warm. I'll fetch the pickup…and Ali…"

"Yes," her whole body was trembling.

"Try not to panic…it's probably not as bad as you think."

When Ali heard Tom's pickup pull up outside she rushed out the door, cradling Daisy, bundled up in blankets, in her arms. Every breath seemed to hold a sob of fear and her heart beat hard at the base of her throat.

He was waiting with the door open, searching Daisy's face in the glow of light from the truck, placing his hand on the mound of her belly to feel for breath. "Her breathing isn't strong but it's regular," he said. "Try not to worry. We'll be there in no time."

For Ali the drive to the hospital seemed to take forever. "Faster, Tom," she begged, glancing across at him. "Please go faster."

His eyes remained focused on the road ahead, but the tense set of his jaw revealed his fears. When the bright lights of the hospital appeared she let out a sigh of relief. "Thank goodness," she cried. "Thank goodness."

To her relief a team was already waiting for them at

A&E. She glanced across at Tom as he pulled up outside. "I rang ahead," he told her, opening the door.

As Ali climbed down from the pickup a nurse reached out to take Daisy. For a moment Ali clung to her child's tiny form, not wanting to give her up, but Tom pried her fingers away.

"Let them help her, Ali," he insisted and with a wracking sob she let her baby go.

The team of doctors and nurses set off up the corridor with Daisy, moving with a professional urgency. "Suspected jaundice," said a young medic to the doctor who had just arrived.

"Keep it down, David," he warned, glancing back at Ali and Tom. "We don't know that yet."

"Did he say jaundice?" Ali clawed her way past Tom to try and catch up with Daisy.

"He said that they didn't know anything for sure," Tom told her, drawing her back. "So try not to worry. She's in good hands now. We just have to stay positive, for Daisy."

"How can I stay positive if my baby has jaundice, she's so young.?" As Ali pressed her hands to her face, tears trickled through her fingers, splashing onto the floor.

"Because as a mother, you have to be strong for your child," Tom said. "You have to believe that everything is going to be fine."

"And if it isn't…?"

"If it isn't…then we'll deal with it."

When they arrived at the small side ward where the medical staff taken Daisy she was already on a drip and a heart monitor bleeped beside her. The nurse blocked the doorway.

"I'm sorry," she said. "But we need to do some checks. I'm afraid you'll have to wait but you can watch your baby through the glass window. The doctor will be as quick as he can I'm sure."

"She's just so tiny," Ali mumbled, watching in horror as they attached wires and tubes to Daisy's motionless body.

Tom placed his arm about her, holding her close. "She's in good hands and she's going to be fine," he told her, with such confidence in his tone that it lifted her spirits.

"She *has* to be fine," cried Ali fiercely, closing her fists so tightly that her fingernails almost brought blood.

"I need to take some details if you don't mind," said a middle-aged nurse with kind eyes. "I know you must be worried but please try and stay calm…if you could just come with me for a moment."

"But I don't want to leave her," Ali cried, hanging back.

"Let the specialist and the doctors do their work and then you can come back and be with your baby," the nurse insisted, motioning to them to sit down in a small seating area.

Ali sat very close to Tom, shivering right down to her core, answering the nurse's questions on automatic; her eyes never left the door to the ward where Daisy was.

"No," she said. "She hasn't shown any signs of being off-color and she's been feeding well… I woke in the middle of the night and… I just knew that something was wrong."

Closing her eyes, she leaned against Tom for support. "She's in good hands," he repeated determinedly. "You'll see…she's going to be fine."

"She has to be," Ali muttered fiercely, trying to convince herself.

"Your husband's right," the nurse agreed. "So try not

to worry. Doctor Harman is with her and he's the best pediatrician there is. Now I'll just go and check on your baby's progress and ask if you can go back in and see her now."

"Sorry…" Ali mumbled as the nurse walked away. "I should have told her that we weren't a couple."

Tom turned his head so that his lips were against her hair. "It doesn't matter," he murmured. "I'm here for you for as long as you need me."

The nurse returned after what seemed an age, accompanied by a tall dark-haired man in a white coat. "This is Doctor Harman," she said. "He'll update you on Daisy's progress."

Ali waited with bated breath. "Please…is she going to be okay?"

"I'm now able to tell youthat we've done the initial tests and although I'm afraid that your baby does have jaundice it is in the early stages so the prognosis is good." Ali crumpled as his words sank in and she would have fallen if Tom hadn't supported her.

"But she is going to be okay?"

"Everything points to that," the doctor told her. "However, she is very young and she's still quite poorly. We need to keep her in the hospital for treatment and we will be doing some more tests. All I can say is please be patient and try not to worry, with the right medication she should soon be on the mend. You'll be able to go back in and be with her very soon."

"Thanks," Ali said, as he disappeared into the ward.

They watched him through the glass, giving out orders to the nurse, who nodded earnestly. When he eventually came back out into the corridor, Ali stepped forward to block his path.

"So is she really going to be okay?" she cried. "Daisy, I mean…my baby."

Doctor Harman cast his dark brown eyes over her, nodding slowly. "As I said, we are doing the best we can. She is stable now and she's sleeping. She is a strong baby and after all our tests I have every hope that she will soon improve…you can sit with her now. I'll see you tomorrow."

"Thank you," Ali cried, rushing into the ward.

The nurse held her back for a moment. "Try not to disturb her," she said in a low voice. "She just needs to sleep."

Daisy lay so still under the special lights used for jaundiced patients, her eyes covered, that at first Ali panicked, until she realized that the baby really was sleeping peacefully. There was a tinge of yellow to her skin but she seemed to be breathing normally.

"You see," Tom said gently. "I told you…she's going to be fine."

Ali looked up at him, her eyes brimming with tears. "Thank you," she said. "For everything."

"She's had some medication," said the nurse. "And she looks better already. You can stay with her here for as long as you like. You're welcome to use the spare bed next to her to get some sleep if you need it."

Ali sank down onto a chair next to her baby, drinking in her tiny form. Chubby arms, still now in sleep, her tiny hands slightly curled.

"She is going to be okay, isn't she," Ali said, glancing up at Tom.

Pushing the hair gently back from her face as if she were a child, he smiled. "You heard what the doctor said. She is a strong baby and there's definitely every possibility that she'll soon be right as rain. Also…"

When he stopped midsentence Ali looked up enquiringly. "Also what?"

"Also…" he went on. "She has a mother who loves her so much that I'm sure that love alone will pull her through. Now I'm going to get you a coffee and something to eat if I can find it, and then I'll probably leave you to it and come back later."

"When?" she asked, not wanting him to go.

"Well…" He looked at his watch. "You rang me at midnight, and believe it or not it's now after six in the morning. The dogs are on their own, remember, so I'll take Freckles back to my place and feed them, then I have to help get *The Sea Hawk* ready for a chartered fishing expedition we're running in a couple of days. I'll call in again this evening though, but you can ring me if you need anything…and Ali?"

"Yes?"

"Try not to worry… I will just go and see if I can find some food for you first though, whether you want it or not. You need to keep your strength up if you're to look after Daisy when she comes home."

WHEN TOM ARRIVED back twenty minutes later, having finally managed to find a coffee machine and a muffin dispenser, Ali was leaning forward, her elbow on the edge of Daisy's incubator and her eyes firmly closed; her skin appeared translucent in sleep and dark rings made shadows beneath her eyes. Daisy, he noted, slept on; her cheeks had more color now and she was breathing rhythmically. She was going to be fine, he knew it.

Placing the coffee and muffin down, he gently eased Ali back in her chair, settling her into a more comfortable position. She murmured in her sleep but her eyes remained closed, so he touched his lips to her forehead and quietly took his leave. On his way he met the nurse; she smiled at him.

"Baby's doing well," she said, "and your wife's asleep, too. Don't worry I'll wake her if there are any problems."

"She's not," he began, and then changed his mind. "Thanks, I need to go now but I'll be back later, oh and…" On impulse he pulled a pen and paper from his pocket and wrote down his number. "Please will you call me if…you know, anything happens."

"Of course," she said, tucking the paper into her pocket. "I'll be going off duty soon but I'll pass the message on to my replacement…and try not to worry. Is it your first?"

Tom nodded awkwardly. "Right, then," he said. "Perhaps I'll see you tonight."

For a moment she frowned. "Oh, so you're going for the whole day."

"I have things to do," he told her. "I'll come straight back if I'm needed."

THE JARRING TONES of her phone woke Ali; she jumped, disorientated. As she felt for it in her pocket, reality dawned. "Oh baby I'm so sorry," she cried, reaching out to Daisy. "How could I have fallen asleep when you're so poorly?"

When Daisy's blue eyes opened and she let out a wail, Ali yelled for the nurse, her heart beating overtime. "Nurse…nurse. She's awake, my baby's awake."

One of the newly arrived day nurses hurried in, talking to the baby softly as she took her pulse and checked her temperature. "This is good," she told Ali with a reassuring smile. "I'll call for the doctor so that he can check her over."

Ali watched through the glass as the doctor did his

checks; when Daisy started crying she went to return to the ward but the small blond nurse stopped her. "Sorry," she said. "Doctor's orders, I'm afraid. He's almost done, though."

When the door swung open again the duty doctor came out into the corridor. "It's good news," he told her. "Daisy's temperature seems to have gone back to normal."

Ali's whole body began to tremble. "Thank goodness...so can she come home?"

"That is up to Doctor Harman but we will need to keep her for a bit longer for further observation and for the jaundice treatment to work. She needs to be feeding normally before we let you take her home too. Doctor Harman will review the situation tomorrow and make a decision then. But try not to worry. Everything does seem to be going well."

Just as the duty doctor left, to Ali's relief, Tom appeared. "Wasn't sure what you'd want," he said, handing over a carrier bag. "So I just brought a few things from the cottage like washing stuff and a couple of items of clothing from your cottage... There's a sausage bap in there too if you're hungry and I've got a flask of coffee here. How's Daisy?"

"Am I pleased to see you," Ali said, smiling at him. "Daisy is doing fine but she'll be in here for a while longer yet so I really appreciate the change of clothes. The nurses here have been really good and they've got me some sandwiches and biscuits but the bap sounds great."

"You stretch your legs have a coffee and maybe freshen up," Tom suggested. "I'll sit with Daisy until you come back."

Doing as she was bid Ali hesitated in the doorway for a moment, looking back to where Tom was leaning forward murmuring to Daisy. It made her feel warm inside to see him like that, showing a softer side she'd never seen before. As soon as she came back he was quick to leave but the warmth stayed with her; he cared, she was sure of it.

IT WASN'T UNTIL late afternoon of the third day that Doctor Harman pronounced Daisy's recovery good enough for Ali to try feeding her with a bottle. She sat in the chair with her baby in her arms feeling like the luckiest woman in the world, Daisy was going to be okay and that was all that mattered.

Ali's phone was on silent and when it vibrated she carefully reached for it.

"It's me, Ali." Lily's cheerful voice in her ear brought comfort. "I told you I'd ring," she went on. "But I haven't been able to get through until now. I've been so worried; is everything okay?"

Ali nodded. "It is now," she said. "Daisy wasn't well so we brought her to the hospital. She's okay now so you don't need to worry."

"Oh poor Daisy," cried Lily. "You sure she's okay?"

"She's fine now, honestly."

"Did you say *we* brought her to the hospital?"

Her voice held a curiosity that made Ali smile. "Yes… Tom drove us here."

"What…in the middle of the night, you mean?"

"Half past midnight to be precise."

For a moment the phone went quiet as Lily absorbed the information. "And is Tom still there with you?" she asked.

"No of course not," Ali responded. "He's been brilliant, though, and he keeps popping in to make sure we're okay."

"But he is coming back later?"

"Look, Lily." Ali decided to set her straight. "You have to put all your ideas about matchmaking out of your head. Tom's been good to me, just like he'd be good to anyone because that's the kind of guy he is, but that's it so don't go getting your hopes up."

Beside her Daisy began mewling like a little kitten and Ali reached out to her.

"Sorry Lily, got to go," she said. "Daisy's just woken up. I'll ring you back later though…and Lily."

"Yes."

"We're both missing you and it's good to hear your voice."

"Missing you, too…don't forget to ring me back."

Ali smiled. "I won't," she promised.

Tom arrived at 6:00 p.m. Ali saw him walking down the corridor, his hair still damp from the shower and his face freshly shaven. He looked so…handsome, she thought, and wholesome and…oh what was she thinking. They'd missed their moment. She appreciated Tom's help so much but, as she'd told Lily, he'd helped her just like he'd have helped anyone because that was just the kind of guy he was and she mustn't start reading too much into it. Still, he had been pretty amazing, keeping her calm and taking decisions when she was a mess.

"Hi," she said appeared round the door. "Glad you could come."

"How's the patient?" he asked, looking down at Daisy, who was sleeping now in her mother's arms. "Better I hope."

Ali's lips quivered as she looked him in the eye. "Daisy's going to be okay…thanks to you."

He shrugged off the compliment, producing a carrier bag with a grand flourish. "Have you eaten?"

"No but you don't need to…" she began.

He raised his hand. "It's just a few sandwiches…and some pie, but it'll keep you going."

"Oh Tom," she said. "Thank you…and thanks for—"

"Look," he cut in. "All I did was to get you here. It's no big deal…anyone could have done the same."

"You were my rock," she said quietly. "And I want to thank you."

"You can tell me when we get Daisy home and we're celebrating," he suggested, his eyes lingering on hers.

"Deal," she agreed. "I'll look forward to it."

CHAPTER TWENTY-THREE

ALI COULDN'T BELIEVE how good it felt to be walking back into the cottage with Daisy in her arms. During their hospital stay she'd tried to stay strong for Daisy, but returning home brought back the awful moment when she'd woken up to find her baby was ill. Tears filled her eyes as emotion flooded in. She'd been so scared for Daisy that night but Tom had made her realize that action was needed, not fear; the action had been all down to him.

Stopping for a moment she glanced back, catching his eye. "You do know that if it hadn't been for you then we might not be coming home today."

"Rubbish," he responded, putting down her bag. "You could have rung a taxi."

"No Tom. I'm indebted to you and I want you to know how grateful I am for all your help."

"I'll put the kettle on," he said, changing the subject. "You go and get the baby settled."

It was an unfamiliar experience, Tom decided, as he brewed the tea, to feel so responsible for someone. He'd always felt a responsibility for his brothers of course, and for Lily, but this was different. Ali and Daisy had no one else to turn to and that added particular challenges for him, especially as he'd already made a firm decision not to get involved with her problems. Now here he was bringing them home from hospital like a regular family…

and the fact that it made him feel good inside was too worrying to contemplate.

When he walked back into the sitting room with two china mugs of tea she looked up and smiled at him and his heart turned over. He didn't need all this tenderness right now; the timing was way out for a start—he had a chartered fishing trip to run very soon and he didn't have time to take on such responsibility. He'd made his decision about where he was going with his life and it didn't include a wife and kids. As far as he was concerned the only sensible thing to do now was to stay well away from Ali. His feelings for her were beginning take a deep hold of him, and if he wasn't careful he wouldn't be able to let her go; he had to nip this in the bud.

"So do you have everything you need?" he asked, putting her mug down on the coffee table and drinking his as quickly as he could. The scalding liquid burned his throat and he spluttered.

"You okay?" she asked.

He nodded. "Yes…thanks. I have to get going, that's all, because we're not ready with the boat yet. I just wanted to make sure you didn't want anything before I go."

Disappointment clouded Ali's brown eyes as she looked up at him. "Do you have to leave so soon? I can make us something to eat if you like."

"No… I mean…thanks, but if you're sure you're going to be okay then I really need to get going."

"Will you call in later?" she asked tentatively. "To bring Freckles home maybe?"

For a moment he hesitated, torn between his heart and his head. His head won. "I'll probably be too late, but don't worry, she'll be fine with me until tomorrow. You could probably do with the break anyway, you have enough on your hands caring for Daisy. Ring me any-time though if you've got a problem."

Ali sat up stiffly, It was clear she had read the signals he was giving out that he wanted space. "I'm sure I won't need to," she said determinedly. "We'll be fine on our own, you go ahead…and thanks for looking after Freckles for me."

He nodded, heading for the door. "No problem. I'll bring her back tomorrow…oh and," for a moment he hesitated. "I did read your book you know…there just doesn't seem to have been a right time to discuss it though, with everything that's gone on."

"And is it the time right now, do you think," she asked. "When you're rushing off?"

He shrugged. "Probably not, I just wanted to tell you how much I loved it."

Color flooded her cheeks. "Thanks," she said slowly. "Perhaps we can talk about it properly when you have more time. I don't want anyone else to read it yet."

"Did your publisher friend like it?"

"He hasn't got back to me so far… I want to ask your advice when he does, you know, about whether to publish it properly or just do some copies for your family."

"You'd do that?"

"I wrote it for you and your family remember, in memory of Bobby. It's up to you what happens to it."

For a moment he just looked at her, drinking in the contours of her face and the way her steaked blond hair fell upon her shoulders, accentuating the soft honey-brown of her eyes. "Thank you," he said.

"You need to go," she told him. "I'll see you soon."

After he left she stayed motionless for a while; *if only, if only, if only* circled around inside her head, until Daisy wailed in her arms, bringing her back to the moment. "It's just you and me now, Daisy," she said determinedly. "In fact there's no room in my life to love anyone else but you…and Freckles of course."

As she stared at the door, though, she had to admit that her heart told a very different story.

TOM WALKED SLOWLY toward The Fisherman's Inn; had Ali seen through his excuse about having to get the boat ready for the chartered fishing trip? The truth was, it was already done. He could have spent the rest of the day with Ali if he'd wanted…and he had wanted. But what you'd like to do and what you felt you should do were two very different things.

As he rounded the corner beyond the stone jetty he stopped in awe to stare at the scene before him. It was awesome to think that people had been looking at this same scene for a couple of hundred years— fishermen like him who sailed the sea for a living and then homed in on the pub for companionship and real ale. Ahead of him the big old whitewashed building was slowly turning gold in the glow of the summer sun. Huge seagulls sat on the picnic tables outside the open door and a gray-haired woman was tending the hanging baskets that buzzed with brilliant color.

"Hello, Mum," he called. "Busy as usual I see."

Grace Roberts turned to look at him, her face lighting up when she saw him. "That is because there's always something to do," she said. "And it's best to keep busy."

Tom nodded, understanding that her grief over Bobby never lessened. "Do you have time for a brew at least?" he asked.

His mother beckoned him over. "Always… I made some scones this morning… You can sample one if you like."

Sitting in the large old-fashioned kitchen with the kettle bubbling merrily took Tom instantly back to his childhood, him and Ned and Bobby growing up with the sea in their blood. Nostalgia hit home. "We were lucky kids," he reflected.

His mother smiled softly, knowing her son. "What's bothering you, Tom?" she asked.

For a moment he hesitated. "The baby's been ill… Ali's baby. I took her to the hospital the other night. They thought it was meningitis but it was a false alarm."

"Poor girl," Grace said. "She must have been distraught."

"She was."

"Are you falling for her, Tom?"

For a moment he hesitated. "No of course not. At least…"

"At least what?"

"I like her, I have to admit that, there's just something about her… That's all it is though. There are way too many complications for it to ever be more than just a friendship… Ned still believes the baby is Bobby's for a start."

Grace sighed, shaking her head slowly. "Ned took Bobby's death hard. I think he blames himself in part for not being able to find him in time, so he tries to lay blame and of course Ali is his main target. Bobby *was* in love with her. I know that because he told me himself, but I believe that as far as she was concerned they were just friends. Accidents happen every day, Tom, and we can't just blame the circumstances. Ali didn't know that her going out on the boat that night would end up in such a tragedy. Ned just wants to make her the scapegoat. And if I am wrong and the baby really is Bobby's, then wouldn't she want us to know it? She has no support now and why would she want to bring it up alone?"

Tom nodded. "Yes, I see what you mean. Ali would want the child's family around."

"I know that she did persuade Bobby to take her out on the boat that night," Grace went on. "And if she hadn't then he'd be here now, so I've had my own issues with blame and anger over that, even though I knew it was wrong. I'll try and talk to Ned again, I think. He's the one who's suffering and he has to try and get past it."

"And have *you*?" Tom asked. "*Really*…got past it I mean?"

Grace looked at him sadly. "I'll never get past the grief and sorrow," she admitted. "But I am getting past the anger, I hope. Anger and bitterness only destroy the bearer and you can't undo what's already been done so you have to try and live with it."

"Do you know, Mum," Tom said thoughtfully. "You're right about the anger and bitterness. I struggled to get past it for a while too…after Bobby… It just seemed so unfair that he was gone and I wanted to lay blame—and then I realized that our job, fishing, putting ourselves at risk night after night in dangerous conditions, was going to cause heartache eventually. I even thought about giving it up for a while until I accepted the fact that fishing and the sea are in my blood. Can't live with it and have a normal life and can't live without it either, I'm afraid… so I guess I'm just destined to be alone."

"If you're telling me that you'd give up on having a wife and family to spare them having to worry about you drowning at sea like Bobby, then you're a fool, Tom," said his mother. "I've been a fisherman's wife for over forty years so don't you think I haven't stayed awake and worried on stormy nights. I'd never have expected your dad to give it up though. It's a part of who he is and I love him for it. Fishing is my life, too, Tom, and I would never change it. When you meet the right woman she'll feel the same way as I do…and if she doesn't then she's not the one for you."

Listening to his mother's wise words Tom felt his heart lighten. "I hope you're right, Mum," he said. "And don't worry about Ned. I'll talk to him again and try to make him see sense."

AS HE WALKED back home later that afternoon Tom hesitated outside Ali's cottage: his mother had really made him question himself today; she was so committed to being a fisherman's wife, so accepting of the danger and the worry it incurred. As far as she was concerned it was a way of life she loved and that was enough to overcome any heartache it might put her through. Was she right though, he couldn't help but wonder. Was it enough or would she have been just as happy with someone else in a less stressful life?

He needed time to sort out his head. He pulled out his phone and tapped out a message, Hi Ali, hope you are okay, please give me a call if you need anything. See you tomorrow.

ALI WAS WATCHING from the window, hoping Tom would come to her door; when her phone pinged and she realized that the message he'd been writing was for her, an emptiness washed over her. It was all well and good to try and come across as strong and independent; the reality however was very different.

Tom slid his phone back into his pocket and glanced across at her cottage one more time before heading off toward home. Had he looked just a little sad and indecisive? she asked herself hopefully. No, she needed to grow up and face facts; she and Daisy were on their own and she had to get used to it.

Watching Tom deliberately walk away without calling in to see her made Ali realize that her suspicions were right and he was avoiding her. Although he'd been so fantastic, taking Daisy to the hospital and looking out for them both, she knew the whole thing had really spooked him and any lingering hopes she had about him having feelings for her were way off. As she walked back toward the kitchen her phone started to ring; she answered it with a flutter of excitement, hoping he'd had second thoughts. "Hi," she said. "I saw you go past..."

"Ali?" Jake's deep voice took her totally by surprise. "What are you talking about?"

She stopped short. "I... I thought you were someone else."

"Obviously."

"What do you want?"

"To talk to my wife," he said. "We aren't officially divorced yet so it is still allowed isn't it?"

Struggling to keep her composure she hesitated for a moment before replying. "No, Jake, it's not," she said. "Because I don't want to talk to you."

"Oh Ali..." He put on his most pleading voice, turning on the charm she used to find so hard to resist. "Okay so I've made a few mistakes but you did ring and tell me about our child so you must still care a little."

"A few mistakes!" she cried. "And I only told you about the baby because I thought it was the right thing to do...and it obviously wasn't so I wish I hadn't bothered."

"Look..." he said. "I'm sorry about the way I reacted but it was a shock, you know, and I was going through a bad patch."

Ali sighed. "When aren't you going through a bad patch, Jake? As far as I'm concerned Daisy has nothing to do with you now…"

"Daisy," he cut in. "That's nice, so we have a daughter called Daisy."

"*I* have a daughter called Daisy," she snapped. "You lost your opportunity to have any input in her life."

"Well to be honest it was a shock at the time and, yes, it did freak me out a bit…but…"

"But what?"

He hesitated then and she knew that he'd be smiling, that broad, disarming smile that always used to bring her round when she was annoyed with him. Now the very thought of it just made her feel even more angry.

"But I've had time to get my head around it now," he said. "And I think I have a right to see my daughter."

"You gave up your rights to Daisy when I told you I was pregnant and you said you weren't interested," she told him, feeling sick. "She doesn't even have your surname."

"But she *is* my daughter?"

With a heavy sigh she gave in. "Yes, she's your daughter. I wouldn't keep that from you…or from her for that matter. She deserves to know who her dad is."

"So you'll let me see her?"

"Only on my terms," Ali reluctantly agreed. "And by prior appointment. Anyway, what about your new girlfriend? I bet she won't be too happy to find out that you're a dad."

"She's long gone," he said. "And good riddance, to be honest. It's you I want, Ali, you and… Daisy. I should never have let you go."

Ali froze, her whole body trembling with anger. "We are over, Jake…for good, so don't even think about it.

You can ring me again and I'll sort out a time for you to see Daisy, but as far as you and I are concerned…we were finished a long time ago."

"Never say never, Ali," he replied, totally unfazed by her outburst. "Who knows, you're all alone with a baby, perhaps you'll find that you do need me after all."

Ali's response was to cut him off. How dare he think for even a minute that she might want to get back with him, after everything he'd done? It was a joke—he was a joke. Turning the phone around in her hand she slammed it down on the table; oh how she wished she'd never made that call to tell him about the baby in the first place.

Daisy's cry broke through the anger that festered inside her, bringing everything back into perspective; she should know by now how good he was at manipulating her and she mustn't let him get to her. She and Jake were in the past, he couldn't hurt her anymore and it was about time he realized it.

Reaching down into Daisy's crib she picked her up and held her close. "Okay, sweetheart," she murmured, touching her lips to her baby soft skin and breathing in her sweet aroma. "Mummy's here—come on, let's get you a bottle."

CHAPTER TWENTY-FOUR

ALMOST NINE O'CLOCK and Tom still hadn't returned home, Ali noted, or at least she hadn't seen him. She'd kept her eye on the window but maybe she'd missed him. He'd have to bring Freckles back at some stage and, when he did, she'd decided to try and talk to him, just to show him where he stood. It was obvious that the whole taking Daisy to the hospital in the middle of the night thing had totally spooked him and she got that. It was hard enough to deal with when it was your own child and Daisy really had nothing to do with Tom…except that he was the one who delivered her. Surely that meant something. She just wanted him to know that she appreciated his help but she expected nothing from him and she wasn't some kind of gold digger or a lonely single mum desperate for a man in her life.

As it happened she didn't see Tom until the next morning when he knocked on her door before 7:00 a.m. She ran down the steep narrow staircase, hair tousled and eyes heavy with the kind of sleep that was crammed in between feeds and a crying baby.

"Oh!" she said, opening the door a crack. "It's you."

"'Fraid so," he said. "Sorry if I disturbed your sleep but I'm out on the boat all day. Snowy's coming with me but I needed to drop Freckles off with you and I was too late to call in last night."

Ali blinked, feeling uncomfortable and wishing that

she'd at least combed her hair. "Sorry," she said, smoothing it down. "I had a bad night with Daisy. I must look a fright."

For a moment Tom hesitated. Did she really not realize just how beautiful she was? "You look great," he told her. "I'm just sorry I had to disturb you so early."

Tightening her brightly patterned robe she pushed the door wider to let Freckles inside. The pup bounded around her, jumping up at her legs, and Ali crouched down to give her a cuddle.

"I've missed you," she said, smiling up at Tom.

And I've missed you, he thought. *Which is exactly why I need to keep my distance.* "Right, then," he said too loudly. "I'd better get on."

Ali stood, smiling at him. "Perhaps I'll see you later?" she said, looking at him expectantly. "Oh and thanks for looking after Freckles."

"No problem," he responded. "But I'm afraid I'll probably be late again so…"

"That's fine," she said too quickly. "You go…"

As Tom hurried off to where his pickup was parked his heart was pounding. He felt like such a jerk. It was for the best though, he was sure of it, despite what his mum said. Trouble was, it was really hard to walk on by every day when she lived just two doors down from him.

LILY ARRIVED AFTER LUNCH. She burst in without knocking as Ali was hanging clothes on the line out in the back yard. "Ali," she called from the kitchen. "I'm back."

Ali went indoors with her laundry basket on her hip and put it down on the table. "Am I glad to see you, Lil," she said, holding out her arms to give the girl a big hug.

Lily hugged her back. "And I've missed you," she cried. "And Daisy…is she all right now?"

Ali nodded "Yes, thank heavens, she's asleep in her crib in the sitting room. You can go check on her if you like but don't disturb her. She needs to sleep."

Following Lily a couple of minutes later, Ali reached down to touch her forefinger to her baby's smooth pink cheek.

"I was terrified when I realized just how ill she was," she told Lily. "But Tom just stayed totally calm—he drove us to the hospital and stayed with us until the doctors had been. Actually he was amazing."

"That—" Lily declared "—is because he likes you."

"Oh Lily." Lost for words Ali just smiled at the open-hearted girl who saw the best in everyone and in every situation. "It's really more because he's a decent, caring man. Don't go getting up your hopes about the two of us being together, Tom doesn't want to take on a woman with a load of history and a newborn baby—in fact I've decided to have a talk to him about it."

"About what?" Lily asked, open-eyed.

"He needs to know that I understand how he feels. It's obvious he's terrified that I'm going to come on to him or something and he couldn't be further from the truth."

Disappointment shadowed Lily's features. "So you don't like him then," she said.

"Of course I like him," Ali objected. "I just don't want him to feel so pressured that he avoids me…and anyway, Daisy and I are okay on our own, we don't need a man in our lives."

"But what about me?" Lily asked sadly. "Don't you need me in your life either?"

"Oh Lily…" Ali hurried to reassure the girl. "I refuse *not* to have you in my life. You're my only friend right now."

"Apart from Tom of course," Lily finished.

For a moment Ali hesitated. Would he still be her friend when she'd spoken to him? she wondered. Or would it be just an excuse for him to back off totally? "I hope he's my friend, Lily," she said, "because that's really all I want of him. I just have to make him realize it."

CHAPTER TWENTY-FIVE

THE SUN WAS high in the sky, the sea glittered as far as the eye could see and a balmy breeze washed over the group of men who stood on the deck of *The Sea Hawk*.

"Perfect day for it," remarked Tom as he steered the boat toward the horizon.

"Don't know about that," Ned grumbled. "None of them have had any experience. They're just going to be hard work if you ask me."

"Chill out, Ned," Tom told him, reaching across to cuff his brother on the shoulder. "All these guys want is a fun day out and the chance to catch a few fish. They're paying us handsomely for the experience so the least we can do is humor them."

"Well I'd far rather be out in a storm catching fish to sell than humoring a load of guys who are just out for a good time," Ned responded.

"You know what, Ned," Tom said. "So would I, although if I'm honest there was a time after Bobby died, when I considered giving it up altogether. I just felt so angry."

"What, you mean angry at the sea?"

"Maybe—I suppose I was confused—then we went out in the boat that day and I knew that I could never give it up. It's wild, unpredictable and dangerous, I know, always will be, but maybe that's what we love best. Today though is about a nice trip out on a sunny day. And it's pretty easy money so don't knock it. Now why don't you go and put out their lunch. By the time they've eaten we'll be at the fishing grounds."

Reluctantly Ned went to do as he was bid and fifteen minutes later the six would-be fishermen were sitting happily tucking into roast beef sandwiches and large portions of pork pie.

"Told you that feeding them was a good idea," remarked Tom as his brother came back into the cabin. "Now I'm just going to let the boat drift while they eat and we can chill out for a bit."

For a few minutes the two men sat in silence; it was Ned who first broke it. "It's obvious that you blame the sea for Bobby's death, Tom, but you're wrong you know. We can manage the sea. It's people who let us down and make our job dangerous."

"By people I suppose you mean Ali," Tom said with a sigh.

"Well, she *was* to blame…and what I can't deal with is that you're still seeing her."

"I'm not *seeing* Ali," Tom responded coldly.

"Well you took her to the hospital."

"Yes, I did…the baby was ill so what else could I do. She's all on her own, Ned, and thankfully I'm not totally selfish… Anyway, she's okay when you get to know her."

"Oh yes and it looks like you've certainly 'gotten to know her'—looks to me as if you've just stepped into Bobby's shoes."

A dull heat flooded Tom's face and Ned must have realized that he'd overstepped the mark. "Sorry. That was a cheap shot."

"About as cheap as it gets," Tom told him. "Look Ned, I think it's about time I gave you a few home truths so sit down, shut up and listen."

"I'm all ears," remarked Ned in a sarcastic tone.

"It's about time you stopped festering in bitterness and got on with your life," Tom began. "I happen to know for a fact that Bobby isn't the father of Ali's baby, and if he had been then she'd have wanted us all to know it and show some support. I also know that although Bobby might have thought he was in love with her, as far as she was concerned they were just good friends. The only person you're hurting with all your bad feeling is yourself, Ned. Your anger is eating you up inside, and to be honest I think you're getting at Ali because you feel guilty for not being able to save Bobby."

"I work for Search and Rescue," Ned butted in, his voice breaking. "I should have been able to find him."

"No, Ned," Tom reached out and took his brother's arm. "If you *could* have saved him then you would have. You're good at your job and if it had been possible to rescue Bobby then you would have done it. You did your best, but sometimes maybe some things are just meant to be. Yes, Ali persuaded him to take her out with us but she couldn't have foreseen what might happen…even Mum has fought her demons and won over that one. The thing is…"

Ned studied his brother, as if trying to take in what he was saying. "The thing is what…?" he asked slowly.

"The thing is," went on Tom, "laying blame isn't really the answer. No one wanted it to happen but it did, it was an awful tragedy but we just have to deal with it and move on with our lives. Maybe even learn from it if we can. It wasn't your fault that you couldn't save him and it wasn't Ali's fault that Bobby fell into the sea. She acted stupidly but she didn't understand how dangerous the sea can be, and Bobby was crazy to launch himself over the edge like that. In fact if you really want to try and blame someone then maybe it should be me. If I'd stuck to my principles and refused to let her come with us, then Bobby would still be alive. I knew it might get rough and yet I let a rookie come out on a fishing trip with us. I was the one in charge and I messed up more than any of you, so maybe I'm the one responsible for Bobby's death. Ali was in my charge, too, and I should have known better than to let her come along."

For what seemed like ages, Ned sat silent, mulling over his confession, Tom figured.

"I never knew you felt like that, Tom," he eventually said. "And maybe you're right about me laying blame to try and ease my own guilt. For what it's worth though I feel a whole heap better for knowing that you've fought your demons, too."

Tom nodded. "I guess we've all learned a lot—just a pity it's too late. One thing is for sure though—no more rookies on *The Sea Hawk*."

Ned grinned, lightening the mood. "What, you men like those rookies over there," he said, gesturing toward the group of eager fishermen. "They're on *The Sea Hawk*, aren't they?"

"Different situation," Tom said. "And as safe as houses. For one, it's not what we consider to be proper fishing, and secondly, we know that they're not going to be in any danger. They're out to have fun and catch some fish. All we have to do is humor them. I know you don't like doing these charters, Ned, but these guys seem decent enough and it's easy money."

"Do you know something, bro?" Ned announced with a smile. "I do believe you're right, so let's get this show on the road."

Tom watched his brother march out on deck with a sense of pride. Ned had always been the sensitive one, the one who took everything to heart. Bobby was just kind of crazy and full of fun, and he…well he was the serious, sensible, boring brother who tried to hold everything together.

"Right, guys," called Ned with an enthusiasm Tom had never seen before. "Who is up for some serious fishing?"

IT WAS OVER two hours later, as the sun drifted slowly down toward the horizon and the sea sparkled crimson and gold, before Tom turned *The Sea Hawk* toward home. Tired but happy and very satisfied with their afternoon's fishing, the men sat on deck, drinking cans of beer with the sea breeze in their faces and arguing companionably about who caught the most fish.

When Ned came into the cabin Tom turned toward him. "Very successful day, Ned," he said. "You did a great job."

Ned shrugged. "I guess I listened to what you said and it kind of made sense. I normally hate these trips but the guys were great… I listened to the other stuff you said, too."

Tom nodded, keeping his eyes on the sea ahead. "And…?"

"And I guess you were right about that, too. I have blamed myself. I beat myself up every day about failing Bobby… I almost handed in my notice at Search and Rescue."

"That's crazy, Ned. You're brilliant at your job, but however hard you try there are always going to be casualties—it's the name of the game."

"That all sounds well and good," Ned agreed. "Until the casualty is your little brother. I should never have laid blame though, it was unprofessional. Anyway…thanks for letting me know how much you struggled after the accident. I didn't realize for a minute that you felt guilty, too. And for what it's worth, Tom, it's not up to me to judge who you want to spend time with."

"Ali really is okay you know," Tom said. "She knows that most people blame her and she understands why. She beats herself up about Bobby, too, you know."

"I had no right go at her the other day," Ned admitted. "It was well out of order."

"Then talk to her," Tom told him. "Go and see her and talk it through properly, tell her exactly how you felt and how you feel now."

"Do you think she knew that Bobby was in love with her?"

"She does now. At the time he was one of her husband's students. As far as I can make out she was all on her own when she and her husband broke up after she found out he'd been cheating on her. Bobby was just a friend, he was there for her and he suggested that she come and stay at The Fisherman's to get material for an article she wanted to write about fishing...for her dad, who died a few months earlier."

"And how do you really feel about her, Tom?"

Tom froze. How *did* he feel about Ali? "To be honest," he admitted. "I'm very drawn to her. It's all just too much though, you know, that deep-rooted guilt and the history she carries around with her like a lead weight... and now there's the baby."

"It's spooked you, hasn't it?" Ned asked. "You know... the thought of maybe having someone to be responsible for."

"Kind of..." Tom admitted reluctantly. "I just don't think it's fair to subject anyone to our way of life, you know, waiting and worrying night after night."

Ned shrugged. "I guess that's up to the person in question, don't you think?"

"Funnily enough," Tom responded thoughtfully, "that's kind of what Mum said. Anyway, enough about all that. I think we should push these charters a bit more now that you've got the hang of them."

"Maybe," agreed Ned. "It's actually been kind of fun today…but coming back to Ali…"

Tom frowned, peering over the wheel. "What about her?"

"You're right, I think I should go and talk to her—and maybe talk to Mum, too. She tried to make me see sense but I just pushed her away…now you've helped me see where she was coming from."

Tom reached across and slapped his hand down on Ned's shoulder. "I'm just glad I've finally gotten through to you… It's time for you to move forward, Ned."

"Yeah," Ned shot his brother a wicked grin. "And maybe it's time for you to move forward, too, Tom. After all, you're no spring chicken anymore."

"Cheeky devil," Tom responded.

"Seriously though," went on Ned. "Don't cut Ali out completely just because of your principles. It's not your decision to decide what people want. Be a friend to her at least, keep an open mind and just see where it goes…"

Tom glanced curiously across at his brother. "You've changed your tune."

"No…" Ned said. "You've changed it for me… Anyway, enough chat, I'll go and get our guests to pack up their stuff, we're nearly home already."

Ahead of them dusk was settling and lights shone out from the harbor, cutting through the half light. *Home*, thought Tom. It was good place to be. He'd think about Ned's advice… Perhaps his brother had actually made some sense. The idea of seeing Ali made his heart race, surely that was a good enough reason not to give up on them just yet. Be her friend, he'd said; it sounded like a good plan...but how to start?

Tonight, he decided. He'd call in tonight on his way home.

ALI TRIED TO concentrate on the TV but the story line evaded her and she jumped up and switched it off, going to check on Daisy for the tenth time in half an hour. The baby slept sweetly, a pink glow of health shining from her perfect face. Leaning down Ali touched her lips to the soft curve of her cheek, gratitude flooding her bones. Things could have been so very different.

Something scratched her leg. Freckles, all wagging tail and smiling face. "Sorry girl," she cried. "I haven't fed you."

As she put the dog bowl down on the kitchen floor, she heard a low knock on the door. Her heart lifted and she pushed her hair back behind her ears self-consciously as she hurried to open it, wishing she'd put on some lipstick.

"Hello," Tom said. "I'm on my way home and I thought I'd stop by and see how Daisy's doing."

"She's fine thanks," Ali responded, not knowing whether to stand back and invite him in or keep him at arm's length as she'd intended. As it happened it was Snowy who decided; pushing between their legs he swaggered inside and ran into the kitchen to finish off Freckles's dinner.

"Sorry," Tom said. "I'll get him." And then he was in her house and the choice was made. As he grabbed hold of Snowy a high-pitched wail sounded from the sitting room and Ali threw him a despairing glance as she went to see to Daisy.

"I'll give Freckles some more food, shall I?" Tom asked, reaching for the empty dog bowl.

Ali nodded. "Thanks… You can put the kettle on, too…if you've time of course."

Ali was sitting on the sofa with Daisy in her arms when Tom appeared from the kitchen. For a moment he just stopped and stared; the expression on her face was just so…loving, he supposed was the only way to describe it. But could he or any man ever compete with the depth of that love, he wondered.

"See," she said, looking up at him with a sweet, soft smile. "She looks fine now, doesn't she?"

"She looks beautiful," he responded. "Like her mum… I mean, she looks so like you."

Ali laughed, amused by his consternation. "I'll take that as a compliment," she said, standing up. "Now if you don't mind holding Daisy for a minute I'll nip and get her bottle."

In one smooth movement Ali passed the baby to him, turning away immediately before he could refuse. "Thanks," she said, disappearing through the door.

Tom held the baby awkwardly, unsure of what to do. "Hey, little one," he murmured, rocking her gently. She stared at him with big blue eyes that seemed to see straight through him and then suddenly she smiled a wide toothless smile; a rush of delight flooded his bones. "Ali," he cried. "Ali, she smiled at me."

"She must like you," Ali said, returning with the bottle. "Would you like to feed her?"

"Oh…" He froze.

"It's okay." Taking Daisy from him, she sat down beside him and held the bottle to the baby's lips. "I don't expect you to take it that far."

"No," Tom said, "I'd like to try feeding her…honestly."

Ali looked at him curiously. "What's brought about this change of heart?" she asked. "You've been avoiding us for the last couple of days and now here you are offering to feed the baby...what's changed, Tom?"

"About that..." Tom caught her eye and then glanced away. "I've been thinking..."

"And?"

"We were, well, almost friends before...and I'd like to think that we can be friends again."

"Oh Tom..." She reached across to place her hand on his arm. "We've never *not* been friends as far as I'm concerned, it's just...well, to be honest I thought that the whole hospital experience must have totally spooked you."

"Actually...it did," he admitted. "Babies are such a huge responsibility...plus there's everything else."

"Like whether you can trust me or not?" she asked.

For a moment he hesitated, but it was long enough to answer her question.

She turned her attention back to Daisy, hiding her face. "Don't bother to make excuses," she said. "I know it's been hard...with Bobby and everything, but I thought we were on the same side with all that now."

"And we are..."

"But you still don't trust me."

"Oh Ali," he placed his hand on hers, holding it tightly. "I do trust you...it's just... You were right about the hospital, it made me think—a baby is such a huge responsibility."

"Well I have a baby...as well you know," she said evenly. "So what are you trying to say?"

"Oh I don't know." With his other hand he reached across to stroke a stray lock of hair from her forehead, looking deep into her warm brown eyes. "We have something, Ali... I'm not sure where it's going yet but I don't want to lose it."

"Me neither," she said, holding his gaze. "And I don't want you to feel that you have to be responsible for us either, so let's just wait and see where it goes...one step at a time?"

"One step at a time then," he agreed. "And this—" wrapping his fingers around the nape of her neck he drew her, unresisting, toward him, brushing his lips against hers "—is my first step."

Ali shivered deep inside, her lips tingling, but instead of taking things any further, he sat back and held out his arms. "And step number two—" he announced "—is feeding the baby."

"Are you sure?" she asked.

His response was just to flash her a pleading smile and determinedly take hold of the bottle. "Well it can't be that hard surely."

As she settled Daisy gently down into his arms Ali glanced sideways at him with a grin. "So I guess step three must be changing her nappy."

"Oh no," he insisted. "I think that's about step twelve. I'm working on step two."

CHAPTER TWENTY-SIX

ALI WOKE IN the night with the sound of Daisy crying in her ears and a warm lump of happiness in her heart. "Mummy's coming, sweetheart," she called, jumping out of bed and walking toward the crib. Last night Tom had kissed her; she touched her fingers to her lips, remembering the feel of his, so soft and gentle. In a euphoric daze she lifted the baby up into her arms, cradling the warmth of her small body. "And he fed you," she murmured, holding her close as she went downstairs to warm a bottle.

When morning light filtered in, however, her daze of happiness seemed to burst, revealing her doubts and weaknesses. Step one had been a gentle kiss that held no passion, step two had been him feeding the baby and step three…step three was merely a suggestion. But were his actions those of a lover or just a friend? Was she reading more into his offer of friendship than he intended? One step at a time, they'd agreed, and she needed to stick to that.

With new resolve, after breakfast she bundled Daisy into a papoose-like sling, took Freckles's lead from the hook by the door and headed out onto the shore. The little dog ran on ahead of her, sniffing along the line of flotsam and jetsam left by last night's tide.

A figure approached from the pathway along the cliff. Ali recognized the man at once and called for Freckles, clipping on her lead. "Come on girl," she urged. "Let's go home."

"Hey…wait," called Ned.

Ali stopped uncertainly. "If you've just come to have another go at me then…"

"It's nothing like that," he said, hurrying toward her. "Honestly."

He stopped in front of her as if cutting off her retreat; his breath came in heaving gasps.

"Then what is it?" she asked curiously.

He shrugged. "I just wanted to talk to you about Tom."

"Tom," she repeated. "What's between me and, Tom, if there is anything at all, is my business."

"He likes you… I get that."

Ali stopped in her tracks. "But we're barely friends so I think you've got the wrong end of the stick altogether."

"Look," Ned shifted from foot to foot. "I may have been a bit quick to judge about everything and…well I guess I want to apologize."

It was only as she exhaled that Ali realized she'd been holding her breath. "Cup of tea?" she asked.

"Make it a coffee and you're on."

It was weird, thought Ali, having Ned Roberts in her tiny kitchen. From the first moment she met him he'd been nothing but judgmental, so why this sudden turnaround in attitude?

"Okay," she said, handing him a mug of strong coffee. "So what's happened to suddenly change your personality?"

He frowned, taking the mug without a thank-you. "There's never been anything wrong with my personality," he insisted. "More just my judgment I suppose you could say."

"Of me you mean?"

"Look," he suggested. "Let's just sit down and I'll try and explain."

Ali sipped her coffee, looking at him with distrust. "Go on then," she said.

"I have to admit I didn't like it when Bobby first brought you here. You were married and much older than him… I didn't want to see him get hurt."

"So you thought I was using him," Ali responded.

Ned didn't seem fazed by her direct approach. "Yes," he admitted. "I thought you were just leading him on because you were lonely and at loose ends. It annoyed me, I guess, and I suppose I was being protective of my little brother…"

"And you blamed me for the accident…for Bobby's death."

"Yes," he admitted. "I did blame you."

"And now you don't?"

"Lily said all along that you and Bobby were just friends but I didn't listen and I should have because she sees things so much clearer that the rest of us…and then Tom made me realize that we were all to blame in one way or another, but accidents happen all the time and it's just circumstance…or maybe fate. I know you didn't intend for Bobby to drown and perhaps I should have been able to find him that night… I let him down, too."

"It was a tragedy, Ned," Ali said. "A terrible, needless tragedy, but there's nothing we can do about it now and hanging on to bitterness and regret will just consume you."

Ned nodded, looking down. "That's kind of what Lily said, too, and then yesterday Tom made me see it… I just wanted you to know that I get it now and I'm sorry for having a go at you."

"And I want you to know that I'll always regret my

stupidity. I should never have gone out on that fishing trip. I've fought my own demons over that one, still do, but I really don't believe that Bobby would want any of us to feel guilty. Sad yes, always will be, but he'd want us to live our lives, Ned."

"You're right," he agreed, putting down his mug. "And, Ali…"

"Yes?"

"Give Tom a chance. You'll never get a better man."

"He's just a friend, Ned, that's all it is."

"I think you might be wrong there… Just promise me that you'll never hurt him."

She smiled then. "I think I may be the one getting hurt," she said. "I have too much history and too much baggage for him to deal with…not that Daisy's baggage of course."

"Can I see her?"

Ned's impulsive request took Ali by surprise. "Why… yes. Come through."

He followed her into the sitting room where Daisy was just blinking off sleep. She stared at them wide-eyed. "See," Ali said, looking at Ned. "She doesn't look at all like Bobby."

"I never expected her to…"

"Are you sure about that? Even Tom took a bit of convincing."

"Honest truth?"

"Honest truth," she repeated.

"I did believe that the baby was Bobby's. Lily told me, Mum told me and…latterly, Tom told me that she definitely wasn't, but I was too twisted up inside to even give you a chance."

"And what's different now?"

"Tom made me see that I felt guilty and I was shift-

ing the blame onto you. It's over, Ali, all that hate, time
to move on."

Reaching up she gave him a quick peck on the cheek.
"Thank you," she told him, "for talking to me... Here."
She went to the desk drawer and took out a copy of *A
Fisherboy's Tale*. "Please read it and let me know what
you think."

"I will," he said. "Thanks."

Before Ali could respond Daisy started to wail and
Ali went across immediately to pick her up.

"See you," Ned said, raising the manuscript in fare-
well. "And thanks."

For a long time after Ned left, Ali sat with Daisy, and
when the bottle was empty still she sat, just holding her.
Ned had insinuated that Tom saw her as more than a
friend, but was he right, and how did she feel about Tom?
One step at a time, she told herself, that's what he'd said
and she mustn't let herself think any further ahead. Still
she watched and waited for his tall straight-backed figure to come marching along the shoreline. The man who
eventually did appear was unexpected, unwelcome and
definitely not Tom.

He wore an expensive raincoat, like the ones he used
to wear when he went climbing. Ali shivered deep inside
as she watched his approach. This was wrong, the timing
was wrong; oh how she wished she'd never told him about
Daisy. Jake's knock on the door was firm and demand-
ing, like him. She didn't want him here right now. Tom
might call in anytime and their relationship was still on
hold; they didn't need any distractions and Jake could be
one huge distraction if he decided to be awkward. Sitting
firm in her chair, she held her breath, desperately hoping
that Daisy would stay quiet. She intended to see him, had
to see him really, and she hated any kind of subterfuge;

he should have rung though, not just turned up like this. As far as she was concerned he could see Daisy but only on her terms; she wasn't prepared to let him just show up unannounced like this.

"Ali," he called, banging on the door. "Ali!"

Guilt made her squirm, but still she ignored him; she'd ring him later and make some arrangements. Now was not the time. When he eventually walked off, she heaved a sigh of relief.

Ali's guilt and embarrassment about hiding from Jake was dispelled minutes later when Tom arrived. What would he have thought, she wondered, if he'd come in to find her ex-husband there? Would they have had a civilized conversation or would Jake have thrown his weight around as only he could? There was a time when she'd admired his arrogance and certainty, mistaking it for strength; for her it had been a big part of her initial attraction…that perceived self-confidence. Now she saw it for what it really was and she was glad she hadn't let him in.

"Hello," Tom said, holding her gaze as he walked in through the door.

One step at a time, she told herself, walking toward him. When he took hold of her hands it seemed natural and right. "Hello," she responded, closing her fingers around his.

He drew her slowly toward him, bit by bit as though afraid that she'd resist, until they were so close that she could feel his breath against her skin, so close that his heart seemed to beat against hers in total harmony, as if they were one being. And when his lips brushed hers in a butterfly kiss she quivered deep inside, reaching up to wrap her fingers around the nape of his neck.

"Oh Ali," he murmured as she drew his lips back

down to hers, meeting their softness with a passion that left them both reeling.

When a loud knock suddenly came on the door they jumped apart. Ali giggled. "We're like a couple of teenagers," she said.

"Ali!" called Lily. "Are you in there?"

"Coming," she responded, self-consciously running her fingers through her hair. As she turned away Tom stepped forward, taking hold of her shoulders to place a kiss against the soft skin of her neck, and for a moment she hesitated, her heart pounding in her ears as she fought off the temptation to just turn into his arms again.

"Ali!" Lily's voice came more urgently now.

"You'd better let her in," Tom said. "She's obviously worried about you."

When Ali opened the door Lily burst into the hallway. "Are you okay?" she asked. "Is Daisy all right?" Suddenly she spotted Tom and a broad smile spread across her face. "He's kissed you, hasn't he," she cried.

Ali glanced at Tom, feeling her face heating, but he just shrugged and raised his eyebrows with an amused smile.

"Don't take any notice, Ali," he said. "Lily's been telling me to kiss you for ages and now she thinks it was all her doing...and anyway, even if I did kiss Ali—" he turned to look meaningfully at Lily "—and I'm not saying I did, then it's our business and it has nothing to do with your nagging."

Lily's blue eyes were bright with excitement. "So... have you fallen in love with him?" she asked.

"I think it takes more than one kiss for people to fall in love," Ali said with an amused smile, very aware that she needed to be totally honest with Tom and determined to tell him about Jake's visit. "You can help me feed Daisy if you like. She'll be waking up any time now. Please, will you just go and see if she's stirring, I need to talk to Tom about something."

"Well?" asked Tom when Lily had left the room. "What is it?"

She looked down at her hands. "I don't want there to be any secrets between us so you need to know that just before you arrived my ex turned up."

"Were you expecting him?"

"No… I told him about Daisy before she was born but he didn't want to know."

"And now?"

"I don't know because I didn't answer the door."

Tom leaned toward her, his eyes dark with concern. "So what if he wants you to give your marriage another go…for Daisy?"

"We're over, Tom. He can see her if he wants to, of course, he's her father, but our marriage is finished."

"Does he drive a big flashy car," Tom asked.

Ali nodded. "Usually."

"Then I think I saw him driving into the village. Perhaps he was looking for accommodation. After all, he isn't going to come all this way and not see you, is he. You'll have to talk to him, Ali, and find out what he wants."

"But I don't want to see him," she insisted.

Tom stood then, calling for Lily. "Perhaps that's because you're afraid of seeing him," he said sadly as his sister appeared in the doorway. "Sorry, Lil," he said. "We need to go. I forgot that I'd arranged to see Dad about something and Mum will be worried about you. Please will you put Snowy's lead on?"

"I *can* come back tomorrow though?"

"Of course you can," Ali said, trying to smile.

"You can leave Snowy here with Freckles if you like, Tom," Ali suggested as Lily ran off to put on his lead. They both knew that she was grasping at straws. "You could call and collect him on your way home."

For a moment Tom held her gaze and a pink flush ran up her throat. "Best if you sort things out with your ex first, Ali," he said. "Make sure you know what you really want."

"I already know," she said but he had turned away.

Ali watched as they walked off together, along the shoreline. Tom so straight and purposeful with the little white dog at his heels and Lily skipping along beside him like a schoolgirl. A flood of emotion rushed over Ali; after everything that had happened, her mother's death, finding her dad and then losing him again, her mess-up of a marriage and the tragedy of Bobby, her pregnancy, finally it had felt as if everything was getting back on track. Lily had asked her if she loved Tom and she'd wanted to say yes because he was the kindest, straightest, most wonderful man she had ever met... And now she had Jake's visit hanging over her; how much more could life throw at her...or maybe she and Tom just weren't meant to be.

As Jake walked back to his car, he was fuming. Why wasn't Ali at home? She had a young baby. She should be there.

He'd imagined this moment, just walking in and taking her by surprise when her guard was down. She'd be mad at him, but he could always talk her round and he'd had his speech all ready.

I know I've messed up, Ali, but you know you've always been the one for me. I may have had a bit of a glitch

*but now I'm really ready to settle down and be a family
with you and Daisy.*

Oh well, he decided, it was only a matter of time. He'd
find somewhere to stay tonight and come back in the
morning. He'd noticed an old pub down in the harbor, or
he could stay at the B&B he'd spotted near the church in
the village center. After deciding to try the pub first he
got into his car and drove slowly through Jenny Brown's
Bay, thinking what a lovely village it was; perhaps he and
Ali could settle down here. Not in that pokey cottage of
course. They could find a proper family house on the
outskirts. Filled with enthusiasm he pulled up outside
The Fisherman's Inn and went inside, leaning his head
down to negotiate the low entrance.

An elderly gray-haired woman was behind the bar.
"Hello," she said. "What can I get you?"

Jake glanced around, noting a group of men at the
other end of the bar drinking lager. "I'll have a pint
please," he said. "And a room and a meal, if that's possible."

"Drink first," she suggested. "And then I'll book you
in and get you a menu."

The three men looked at him curiously and he raised
his glass. "You must be locals," he said. "Do any of you
know Ali Nicholas? She has a young baby, Daisy?"

CHAPTER TWENTY-SEVEN

WALKING SLOWLY HOMEWARD with the evening sun on his back and a song on his lips for the first time in over a year, Ned thought about the talk he'd had with Tom. It had really made him see things differently and helped him face up to a lot of stuff—demons, he supposed they were, things he'd struggled to come to terms with. Now that he'd gone to see Ali, he felt as if he'd really got past all that. He'd misjudged her, he knew that now, and he'd laid all the blame at her door when he, too, had been guilty. He felt so much better after their conversation, as if he'd actually done something to feel proud of. Maybe it was time for him to get back to the way life was before, even perhaps have a little fun again.

On a sudden impulse he pulled out his phone and scrolled down to Nick's number. "Hi Nick…its Ned. Fancy a night out tonight, just a few pints at The Fisherman's… We could even go into town later if you fancy it. Give Harry a call, too, if you like."

The answer came at once. "Bit late for that, Ned, we're already here. Hurry up and get yourself spruced up. We'll order you a pint. It's about time you joined us on a night out again."

The three friends were on their second drink when the stranger came in to the pub. He looked sure of himself, assertive and well dressed, definitely not a fisherman or a farmer. Ned heard him trying to book a room and then he raised a glass to them and asked them about Ali.

Ned turned cold inside and Harry cast him a quick glance. "Might do," he said. "What's she to you anyway?"

The man took a long swig of his drink and looked at them with an arrogance that made Ned's blood boil. "She's my wife and Daisy is my daughter. I've come to take them home."

When Ned stepped forward Nick placed a restraining hand on his arm, knowing his friend only too well. "Leave it, Ned," he said in a low voice. "Just get the facts first."

Leaving his companions at the bar, Ned went to find Tom, wondering what was going on. Had he finally accepted Ali only to find out that she really was a two-timing schemer after all, someone who just used people for her own ends as he'd first suspected? It would break Tom's heart.

His mum was in the back, working in the kitchen. "Have you seen Tom?" he asked.

She shook her head, concerned at the expression on her son's face. She knew how much he'd been struggling, but according to Tom he was over it now. "He should be here soon though," she said. "He's bringing Lily back and he wanted to talk to your dad about a problem with the boat… What's up anyway?"

For a moment Ned hesitated, wanting to offload his worries; no point in upsetting his mum, though, he decided, at least not until he was sure. "Nothing," he said. "It's nothing important. If you see him before I do, will you tell him I need to talk with him?"

"Yes of course," she agreed with a puzzled frown. Would there ever be a time when she didn't need to worry about her sons, she wondered.

Ned saw Tom and Lily approaching as soon as he stepped outside. Something about the expression on his brother's face rang alarm bells in his head. "Tom," he called. "Do you have a minute? I need to talk to you about something."

Tom stopped. "You go on," he said to Lily before turning back to Ned. "Okay," he said. "What is it?"

As Ned reluctantly told him that Ali's ex was in the bar Tom cursed under his breath. "She told me he was here," he said. "But she said she didn't want to see him…"

"I'm sorry, Tom." Ned reached across to give his brother a sympathetic pat on the shoulder. "But I don't think that's how he sees it. He was bragging about how he's come to take them home… Perhaps you should just go and ask him what he's about."

"Too right I will," Tom agreed, heading off into the pub.

Jake was still at the bar, complaining that his food was taking too long.

"I believe you're looking for Ali," Tom said, stepping up beside him.

"My wife you mean," Jake responded, glaring at him. "How do you know her?"

Tom hesitated for a moment. "She's a friend of mine."

"Not too good a friend, I hope," Jake remarked with an amused, arrogant smile. "I've come to get her and the baby. We're going to be a real family now and…"

"She told me you were over and your divorce will be through at any time," Tom cut in.

Jake just shrugged. "Well you can't be that good a friend or you'd know how fickle Ali is. She's on and off with everyone but she always comes back to me eventually. This time we're going to really try and make a go of it…for Daisy."

"I don't believe you," Tom told him, longing to wipe the smug smile off his handsome face.

"Believe what you like but I *was* round at her cottage earlier and I'm going back there later on…to talk about *our* future."

"I don't believe that you have a future with Ali," Tom said.

Jake shrugged. "Think what you like but it really has nothing to do with you."

Anger bubbled as Tom forced himself to turn and walk away.

"I'm so sorry bro," Ned said, "Perhaps we got Ali wrong after all…"

Tom set his jaw. "No, Ned… Ali told me it was over with him and I really believe she thinks it is. There's a baby to consider in all this though. Whether I like it or not he is Daisy's dad and Ali has to be sure… So I'm not going to interfere."

"But don't you think you should fight for her if you really care?" Ned asked.

Tom looked his brother in the eye, wanting to be honest. "The thing is, Ned… I believe her now, about Bobby and about her ex. It's just…"

"What, Tom, it's just what?"

"Oh I don't know. To be honest, if it did go somewhere with Ali and me I'm still not really sure that I could ever expect her to be the wife of a fisherman. Let's face it, Ned, it would be a life darkened by worry and possibly grief. She's a journalist and he's wealthy and successful, they're far better suited than Ali and I will ever be. Even if we did get together, she'd probably end up regretting it."

"If you're having doubts about her then…" Ned began.

"I don't have doubts about my feelings for her," cut in

Tom. "It's the other way round… I'm just not sure if she really knows what she wants."

Tom said goodbye to his brother and left the pub, more confused than ever. Talking to Ned had made him face up to all his doubts—about Ali, about himself and about his way of life.

He'd go and see his dad. Talking boats and fishing always took his mind off his problems; when he finally set off for home, just after nine, his head was still full of doubts and recriminations.

AFTER TOM AND Lily left, Ali made sure that Daisy was settled and then sat and waited for Tom to come past on his way home. He might not intend on stopping by but she had to make him listen to her, had to make him see that she and Jake really were over. If necessary she'd wait all night.

Darkness fell and outside Ali could hear the swish of the tide rushing up the shore, but still there was no sign of Tom. Daisy mewled in her crib, like a little kitten wanting attention, and Ali gently stroked her baby-soft hair back from her face. Daisy had just slipped back to sleep when she heard a knock on the door. Jumping up, her heart echoing in her ears, she ran to answer it… So he had stopped by after all.

"Hello," said Jake as she flung the door wide. "I've come to see my daughter."

She moved forward to block him but he stepped boldly around her.

"Aren't you going to put the kettle on?" he asked. "We have a lot to talk about."

"How dare you just walk into my house," cried Ali, as Jake marched inside and shut the door behind him. "You have no right."

He looked at her with an amused smile. "I have every right. You are my wife and the mother of my baby... Where is she by the way?"

"It's over between us, Jake, I told you that. You are Daisy's dad and you can see her, on my terms, but you have no right to just come walking into my life like this. I want you to leave right now and I'll sort out a suitable time for you to meet her."

"No time like the present," Jake said. "Come on, Ali, you owe me that at least."

"I owe you nothing, Jake," Ali said, picking up her phone. "And if you don't stop harassing me then I'll call the police."

"Oh Ali..." Jake stood in front of her, sounding sad and morose. "We were in love once, don't you remember? Surely you don't begrudge me seeing the child that was born of our love."

Panic flooded over Ali; he had no right to make her feel guilty, no right to just invade her privacy like this. "You can see Daisy and then I want you to leave," she said.

As if on cue Daisy began to cry. Jake hurried toward the sound, stopping next to the baby's crib to stare at her in awe. "Let's get back together, Ali," he said, reaching across to take her arm. "We were good together once and now we can be a real family... All that...stuff, was just a midlife crisis, it meant nothing to me. This—this is real."

"No, Jake," she insisted. "We're over and you'll just have to get used to it."

"Well then just let me feed her," he pleaded. "Let me hold my daughter in my arms and give her a bottle...then I'll leave, for now."

"When you see Daisy again, it's on my terms only,

Jake," she said. "I set the rules; I already told you that. You can give her a bottle and then you have to go."

As he sat down on the settee and took Daisy in his arms, Ali stood impatiently and waited for Jake to get tired of the job. Daisy took her milk greedily, sucking hard on the nipple until it was gone. Ali rushed to take the bottle as soon as it was empty. "There," she said. "I'll take her now."

When she reached out her arms Jake ignored her, refusing to let go. "Please, Jake," she said. "She needs changing…give her to me."

He lifted her up against his chest when it happened. One minute there he was, all smart and tidy in his stylish clothes, and in the next spit-up covered his chest and jacket.

Ali wanted to laugh, wanted to tell him it served him right, but she bit her lip and took the baby. "I'll just see to Daisy and then I'll do something about your clothes," she said.

"Never mind the baby," he roared, "Get this stinking vomit off me…now."

"Baby comes first," Ali told him, hiding a smile. "This is just part of being a parent."

"Tell you what, Ali," he said coldly, standing up. "Maybe I'll come another day. I wanted to give us another chance but I can see that trying to convince you tonight is just a waste of time."

Ali stood, Daisy in her arms. "Tell me the truth, Jake," she said. "I know you too well to believe that you've come back here to try and be a family man when you've never wanted kids. What is it really…money perhaps?"

To Ali's surprise he seemed to shrink before her. "If you must know I've been made redundant," he admitted, looking anywhere but at her. "And I've let a couple of mortgage payments slip... Truth is I'm in trouble, Ali."

"Oh Jake," she responded, touched by his obvious distress. "Why couldn't you just be honest with me in the first place? We might be over but that doesn't mean I don't respect what we once had. If money is the problem then that's easily solved. Look... I don't care about the house and I'll never come back to live in the city so why don't we just renegotiate the settlement so that you keep it?"

Jake frowned. "And what do you get out of it?"

"All rights to my daughter...and peace of mind. Sell it right away and rent somewhere until you get another job. And you will get another, trust me. You just have to put in the effort. Now give me a minute to see to Daisy and then I'll clean you up a bit before you go."

"And you really did mean it, about the house I mean?"

"Of course I meant it. It's just a house and there are more important things than money. Now tell me the truth, Jake, do you still want to play a part in Daisy's life?"

"To be honest, I'm not really sure I'm the fatherly type," he said, pulling a face at the wet patch on his chest. "But that doesn't mean I don't want *some* involvement. I mean, I want my daughter to know who I am at least."

Ali nodded, relieved that he was willing to take a back seat. "That's fine with me. Sort out your finances and your job and then we'll see where we are...agreed?"

"Agreed," Jake said. "And Ali..."

"Yes."

"Thanks."

CHAPTER TWENTY-EIGHT

ALI SLEPT FITFULLY, waking up again and again and wishing she'd had the chance to talk to Tom; when morning dawned drizzly and cool it seemed to reflect her mood. After seeing to Daisy and feeding Freckles she reached for her phone and scrolled down to Tom's number, hesitating before calling him; after all she didn't want him to think she was desperate and needy. She'd just wait, she decided, and see what happened.

It was almost lunchtime when Lily called. She burst in bright and breezy as usual. "Seen Tom?" Ali casually asked.

Lily frowned. "He was with Ned and some friends in the pub last night and I heard Ned later on from my window. He was outside talking to one of his friends about someone in the bar who'd upset them."

"Oh dear… Who was it, do you think?"

Lily shrugged. "I think he was staying at the pub. Ned said he'd come to see his wife… Can I go see Daisy now?"

Ali smiled while inside her heart was sinking. "Of course. Don't disturb her if she's still asleep though."

TOM STRODE BY at twelve fifteen staring straight ahead as he passed by Ali's door; he looked tired and unkempt she thought, as if he hadn't bothered to shave.

"You okay, Tom?" she called, determined not to let him ignore her.

When he hesitated she ran to catch him up. "What is it, Tom… Have I done something wrong—is this all about Jake? I know he stayed at the pub last night."

"I saw him here when I was on my way home last night."

"Is that why you're angry with me, Tom? But why? I told you he'd been here and you knew he'd come back. I thought you trusted me."

For a moment he seemed to weaken. "Oh Ali," he cried, reaching out to touch her cheek with his forefinger as if afraid of making any more contact than that. "I do trust you. That's not the issue."

"Well what is the issue then?" she pleaded. "Yesterday we were…yesterday I thought. What's changed, Tom?"

"I don't know, Ali," he admitted. "There are just too many issues, that's the trouble. For a start, you aren't meant to be stuck in a fishing village waiting and worrying for a husband that might not come home. Seeing your ex has made me realize what kind of life you used to live and it's not this."

"You are so wrong, Tom," Ali said sadly.

"Maybe I am," he told her, "And I hope you're right, but right now I need some space."

Lily was in the hallway when Ali went back into the cottage. She tried to brush away her tears, too late. "I know you and Tom have had a row," she said. "So you may as well come into the kitchen and tell me what's going on. And Daisy's fine so you don't need to worry about her."

Ali sat at the kitchen table with her head in her hands. "I love him, Lily," she said. "That's the trouble… And I thought he was falling in love with me."

"He was… I mean…is," responded Lily. "Look, I know it has something to do with last night so just tell me… I'm eighteen now you know, not seven."

Ali reached across to place her hand on Lily's arm. "I know you are," she said. "And I don't know what I would do without you."

"Then tell me?"

"Did you see the man last night," she asked. "The man who stopped at the pub?"

Lily nodded. "Yes…fleetingly. He was quite tall, and dark haired."

"And suave and sophisticated," Ali added.

"Well…yes, I guess."

"He was my ex and he called in to see me, but we really are over, Lily. Do you believe me?"

"Yes," Lily said with no hesitation. "Of course I believe you and I know that you love Tom."

Ali looked at her. "Tom's got some idea in his head about it not being fair for me to live here in the village and be a fisherman's wife. He said he needed space, Lily, and I'm going to give it to him. Oh I don't know, maybe we're just destined not to be."

"You are destined to be together," Lily cried. "I know you are and somehow we're going to make Tom see that. I have to go now but I'll be back tomorrow…and Ali…"

"Yes."

"You love each other and surely that's the most important thing…so never give up."

"I don't think Tom sees it quite like that," Ali said, trying to smile.

Those three words, *never give up*, went round and round in Ali's head as she nursed Daisy, rocking her to and fro in her arms and pressing her lips against the sweet baby softness of her skin. And they were still circling in her head when she woke in the night, moving from sleep to full awareness in just a second. *Never give up... never give up...never give up.* Slipping out of her bed she checked on Daisy and ran down the stairs to make tea; Lily was right, she realized; she mustn't give up.

Sipping her drink she switched on her computer and went into Documents, scrolling down to *A Fisherboy's Tale* and clicking on Print.

When Lily arrived at ten o'clock the next morning Ali was carefully putting copies of her book in colored files. "Morning," she called. "Here, Lily, please will you make sure that both your mum and your dad get a copy of this, and ask Tom and Ned to make sure they've read theirs... Here," she handed a copy to Lily. "This is for you, I know you don't really do much reading but please just try and read it for me."

"Course I will," Lily agreed. "But why, Ali... Has it got to do with Tom?"

Ali nodded. "Yes...hopefully. Maybe reading this will make everyone realize just how much I really do care. When did you say the memorial for Bobby was?"

Lily frowned. "This Saturday night. It's a party though not a memorial, it would have been his birthday soon and it's going to be a celebration... Why do you ask? What are you planning?"

"You'll just have to wait and see," Ali said, smiling. "Let's just say it's an all or nothing effort... Don't breathe a word though."

FOR THE NEXT few days Ali kept herself to herself. To her relief she didn't hear from Jake. Lily came and went as usual and Tom walked past her cottage each day but she determinedly didn't try and attract his attention, wanting him to trust her again of his own volition.

"Did you tell all your family to read my book, Lily?" she asked on Friday.

Lily nodded. "I saw Mum reading it last night and Ned's copy is open by his bed. I don't know about Dad."

"And the memorial party tomorrow night starts at seven thirty?"

"Yes… It's in the big back room at the pub and it's going to be all about remembering Bobby and celebrating his birthday… Why, are you coming?"

"Tell you what, Lily," Ali said, leaning toward her. "If I let you in on a secret will you keep it?"

"Of course," declared Lily. "I'm good at secrets."

CHAPTER TWENTY-NINE

SATURDAY DAWNED BRIGHT and clear. Ali woke with fresh hope tinged by apprehension; what if she made a fool of herself? Pushing any negativity from her mind she fed Daisy and by eight thirty she was walking along the shore with the baby in a sling while Freckles ran in front of them, sniffing out any interesting scents she could find.

The air was fresh and clear with a definite autumnal nip. Ali breathed in deeply, taking in the scents and sounds of the sea as it rushed up the shore, trying to think of anything other than tonight, when in truth it was the only thing inside her head. As she reached the top of the cliff path she stopped and looked back. She could see Cove Cottages way below her, perched almost at the edge of the sand but securely built on limestone rock. Someone was walking along in front of the cottages; the breath caught in her throat and her heart beat overtime. It was Tom—Tom and Snowy heading past her cottage. Would he stop and look to see if she was there?

He hesitated, calling for Snowy, or pretending to and then he went on his way, walking quickly. Was there really any point in tonight, she wondered, or was she just going to look like a fool? "Oh Daisy," she said, leaning down to touch her lips to the baby's head. "I think that Mummy might be making a big mistake."

Heading back toward her cottage she tried to hang on to the positivity she'd felt when she outlined her idea to

Lily. It had taken months for Tom to finally begin to believe in her and now even Ned had come around...until Jake turned up and made Tom question everything. *Never give up*, Lily told her, but despite those three brave words doubts began to invade her determination; perhaps she should just give up on loving Tom and walk away.

That was impossible, though, she realized, for true love didn't let go of you that easily and she wasn't ready yet to give in gracefully either. Perhaps Tom didn't love her enough to overcome his issues but at least she'd have given it her best shot. Tonight, she decided, she really was going to go all out for it. After that she didn't care.

For almost an hour Ali went through her wardrobe, changing from one outfit to another and back again. She wanted to look her best, to appear honest and reliable. In the end she chose a simple blue above-the-knee dress that showed off her slim, tanned legs, with navy heels for that bit of elegance. She even took longer deciding what Daisy should wear, but by eight o'clock they were ready. Loading the baby into her car seat she almost had second thoughts.

"It's our one last chance, Daisy," she said determinedly, tucking her blanket around her. "And all I have to do now is speak from the heart and hope."

Ali hadn't realized how busy Bobby's memorial would be. Of course, he'd been a very popular character around here so obviously there were going to be lots of people who wanted to come and remember him.

The sound of laughter trickled through the bar from the function room at the back of the pub. Holding Daisy close for comfort, she took a deep breath and headed for the doorway. She'd timed it so that the tributes to Bobby were finished and the food was about to be served. That way she could get everyone's attention.

Lily was waiting by the door. "Just a few more minutes," she said. "Dad's about to say something about Bobby and then I'm going to step up and tell them that there's one more person wanting to speak."

Ali looked around nervously. "Do you know if they read the book?"

Lily nodded eagerly. "Yes and they loved it. Mum was crying and even Dad shed a few tears when he finished it… It's going to be okay, Ali, I know it."

"I wish I was as confident as you," Ali groaned. "This is beginning to feel like a really bad idea."

"No it's not," Lily insisted. "Look, Dad's nearly finished… I'm going in now, Ali. You ready?"

"Well I'll never be ready but I am going to give it my best shot."

A hush fell over the room as Jed Roberts went to sit down and Lily took the moment to announce another speaker. When Ali walked in clutching Daisy in her arms a low rumble of surprise rippled through the gathered crowd. Ignoring it, Ali walked to the front of the room with her head held high.

"I am here," she began. "Because, like all of you, I cared for Bobby…as a good friend. He helped me when I was in a bad place and I would do anything to undo what happened that day on the boat. I wrote *A Fisherboy's Tale* for all the Roberts family. I wrote it from the heart in memory of Bobby so that we can all read it and remember him forever."

Ali hesitated then, glancing across at Tom; their eyes met briefly but the connection lasted merely a second before he looked away. She took a deep breath, trying to control the rapid beating of her heart. "*A Fisherboy's*

Tale has also been read by an editor from one of the big publishing houses," she went on. "He is keen to publish it in book form but as I have officially handed the ownership of the book to Jed, Grace, Tom, Ned and Lily, what happens to it now is their decision. It can stay just within the family or, if they choose, it can be published and any money it makes could be used to do something that Bobby would have wanted."

A ripple of appreciation ran around the room at her words, but she lifted her hand to stop it.

"I don't want thanks," she said. "It's a small thing to do for Bobby after the enormity of the tragedy that ended his life…and I'll always feel some responsibility for that. For what it's worth, I know I should never have gone on the boat that day and I'd do anything to undo what happened… This is a small gesture I know, but it's all I have."

The room fell silent then, all eyes on Ali as she spoke from the heart. "I came here, to Jenny Brown's Bay, on Bobby's suggestion, to try and get my head straight about my marriage breakdown. I didn't know when I came here that I was going to be a mum and I don't know how Daisy survived my fall into the ocean, but she did and she's here and I love her. My marriage is over forever and I love the way of life here in Jenny Brown's Bay, Tom, no matter what you may think."

Everyone turned then to look at Tom, who was staring at her in shock. Ned and Jed stepped up beside him to stop him from making any attempt to leave, and as Ali looked at him across the room with her heart in her eyes, somehow he couldn't look away.

"I also want you to know, Tom Roberts," she said. "In front of all your friends and family—I love you with all my heart, and if you still have doubts about me then I swear that I never have and never will be untrue. I hope Bobby's book can make a difference in some way and… and, Tom, with…or without me, I hope you find happiness."

When the whole room went suddenly silent she felt the pressure of tears behind her eyes. She'd read the situation all wrong and behaved like a fool. A gasp rippled around the room as she turned and fled with Daisy clutched close against her chest and tears rolling down her face.

Grace and Lily were the first to move. "Tom," Grace pleaded. "Make this right."

It was full dark when Ali ran out into the night, with not even the sliver of a moon to break through the shadows. She hadn't thought about what would happen after she had her say, but she hadn't reckoned with that awful shocked silence either. They were probably all laughing now at her needy, pathetic speech.

Grace appeared beside Ali as she fumbled for her car keys, placing her hand firmly on her shoulder. "Let me take Daisy," she said. "Please. You and Tom need to talk."

"No," Ali turned determinedly back toward her car, her fingers shaking as she withdrew her key. "It's too late… All I've done is to make a fool of myself. I should have just left without saying anything."

"Give the baby to me," Grace repeated, holding out her arms. "I'll look after her so you don't need to worry. You have to see this through."

Silently Ali handed Daisy over. "But what if…" she began.

"Just go and find him," Grace urged. "And Ali…"

"Yes…?" Her whole body trembled.

"We all loved the book. Thank you so much for the memories."

As Grace went back inside with Daisy, Ali stepped

into the shadows. What if he didn't want to talk to her? What if he didn't even come and she had to walk back inside to get Daisy and face all those people.

A beam of light cut through the darkness as the door to the pub opened and suddenly there he was, his familiar figure outlined by its warm yellow glow. Ali stood motionless in the darkness, a tide of emotion rising inside her. He stepped forward, looking around. "Ali," he called. "I'm… I'm sorry…"

To Ali it felt as if a dam had burst inside her. She stepped into the light, her eyes focused on his face. "It's I who should be sorry," she said quietly.

His response was to open his arms and she walked into them as if it was the most natural thing in the world. "Oh Ali," he murmured as she laid her head against his shoulder, breathing in his fresh, spicy scent. "It was so brave…your speech, and it made me feel so ashamed. I should have trusted you…trusted us."

Drawing back, she looked up into his eyes. "Do you trust us now?" she asked.

He cupped her face between his hands. "To the end of the earth and back," he said, touching his lips to hers.

She responded by gently returning his kiss. "I love you, Tom Roberts," she whispered. "I think I've loved you forever and I'm so sorry for all the trouble I've caused."

He held her close against his heart. "I love you, Ali Nicholas, more than you know, and it was life that caused the troubles we've had, not you. The past is behind us now, though, it's tomorrow that really counts. I know that now and I know with every part of me that I want to spend all my tomorrows with you…so…" He looked down into her face with a dark intensity in his eyes.

"So… What?"

"Marry me…please, Ali. You and Daisy, I just want us to be a family and…"

Gently she placed her fingers over his lips. "Stop rambling, Tom, and kiss me."

He wrapped his arms tightly around her, holding her so close that she felt as if they were one being, and she let out a sigh of pure happiness. In the moment when his lips reached hers, she held back, smiling up at him. "Yes, yes, yes," she cried. "I will marry you, Tom. I love you to the moon and back and I'm never going to let you go again."

His lips finally found hers with a passion that left her breathless. "And now," he said, taking her hand and drawing her back toward the pub. "Let's go find our baby and tell everyone our news."

They were met by cheers and hoots of joy from the crowd that had gathered outside, and in front of them all Tom kissed her again before putting his arm about her shoulders and turning to face them. "I'd like you all to meet my wife-to-be," he said, looking at Ali with such pride that she felt the tears begin again.

Finally, she realized, she was home.

* * * * *

MILLS & BOON

Coming next month

CINDERELLA'S NEW YORK CHRISTMAS
Scarlet Wilson

Leo finished the call. New York. He'd wanted to go back there for days. But somehow he knew when he got there, the chances of getting a flight back to Mont Coeur to spend Christmas with his new family would get slimmer and slimmer.

Here, he'd had the benefit of a little time. Everything in New York was generally about work, even down to the Christmas charity ball he was obligated to attend. As soon as he returned to the States...

His stomach clenched. The Christmas ball. The place he always took a date.

For the first time, the prospect of consulting his little black book suddenly didn't seem so appealing.

'Nearly done.' Anissa smiled as he approached.

'I have to go back to New York.'

Her face fell. 'What?'

She was upset. He hated that. He hated that fleeting look of hurt in her eyes.

'It's business. A particularly tricky deal.'

Anissa pressed her lips tight together and nodded automatically.

The seed of an idea that had partially formed outside burst into full bloom in his head. He hated that flicker of pain he'd seen in her eyes when she'd talked about being in Mont Coeur and being permanently reminded of what she'd lost.

Maybe, just maybe he could change things for her. Put a little sparkle and hope back into her eyes. Something that he ached to feel in his life too.

'Come with me.' The words flew out of his mouth.

Her eyes widened. 'What?'

He nodded, as it all started to make sense in his head. 'You said you've never really had a proper holiday. Come with me. Come and see New York. You'll love it in winter. I can take you sightseeing.'

Anissa's mouth was open. 'But…my job. I have lessons booked. I have chalets to clean.'

He moved closer to her. 'Leave them. See if someone can cover. I have a Christmas ball to attend and I'd love it if you could come with me.' His hands ached to reach for her, but he held himself back. 'I called you Ice Princess before, how do you feel about being Cinderella?'

He could see her hesitation. See her worries.

But her pale blue eyes met his. There was still a little sparkle there. Still a little hope for him.

Her lips turned upwards. 'Okay,' she whispered back as he bent to kiss her.

Continue reading
CINDERELLA'S NEW YORK CHRISTMAS
Scarlet Wilson

Available next month
www.millsandboon.co.uk

COMING SOON!

We really hope you enjoyed reading this book. If you're looking for more romance, be sure to head to the shops when new books are available on

Thursday
4th October

To see which titles are coming soon, please visit
millsandboon.co.uk

LET'S TALK
Romance

For exclusive extracts, competitions
and special offers, find us online:

f facebook.com/millsandboon

⊙ @millsandboonuk

𝕏 @millsandboon

Or get in touch on 0844 844 1351*

For all the latest titles coming soon, visit
millsandboon.co.uk/nextmonth